Hallie Marsh Mysteries

6

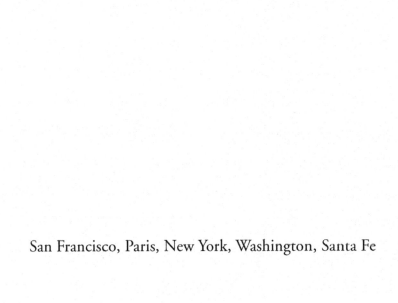

San Francisco, Paris, New York, Washington, Santa Fe

Merla Zellerbach

21 Huntington Court

firefall™

First Edition: February 2015

cover design: BJR/EB/SES
cover photo: A.M. Schmoltner

hardcover: 978-1-939434-92-0
paperback: 978-1-939434-90-6

FIREFALL EDITIONS
Canyon California 94516-0189
literary@att.net
www.firefallmedia.com

Library of Congress Cataloging-in-Publication Data

Zellerbach, Merla.
  21 Huntington Court / by Merla Zellerbach. -- First edition.
    pages ; cm. -- (Hallie Marsh mysteries ; 6)
  ISBN 978-1-939434-92-0
  I. Title. II. Title: Twenty-one Huntington Court.
  PS3576.E446A614 2015
  813'.54--dc23
                              2014035117

Novels by Merla Zellerbach

21 Huntington Court

The A-List Murders

Dying To Dance

Love To Die For

The Missing Mother

Mystery of the Mermaid

Secrets in Time

Firefall Editions

Rittenhouse Square

Random House

Sugar

Cavett Manor

Love The Giver

The Wildes Of Nob Hill

Ballantine

Love In A Dark House

Doubleday

I HUMBLY acknowledge some of the many friends, acquaintances, and relatives who have helped and encouraged me along the way:

Alphabetically: Judge Angela Bradstreet & Cherie Larson, Anne & Roger Walther, Barbara Schraeger & Phil Plant, Belva Davis & Bill Moore, Beth Townsend, Brenda Payton, Chandra & Bob Friese, Charlotte & George Shultz, Cissie Swig, Clarissa Dyer, Dagmar Dolby, Debra Dooley, Dede Wilsey, Delia Ehrlich, Sen. Dianne Feinstein & Sir Richard Blum, Ellen & Charles LaFollette, Ellen Newman, Fran & Bud Johns, Françoise & Andy Skurman, Gretchen de Baubigny, Helen Hilton Raiser, Ingrid Nystrom, JaMel & Tom Perkins, Jennifer Raiser, Judge Katherine Feinstein & Señor Rick Mariano, Linda & Steve Millard, Lisa & Doug Goldman, Lisa & John Grotts, Lucie & Jerry Weissman, Dr. Madeline Levine & Dr. Lee Schwartz, Margot Schevill, Mary & Bill Poland, Maryann & Jack Opperman, Nancy & Joaquim Bechtle, Nancy Livingston & Fred Levin, Pamala & Ted Deikel, Pat & Jerry Dodson, Pat Montandon, Sharon Litsky & John Sampson. More thanks to Paula Taubman and my friends at Compassion & Choices, my pals at the Chronicle: Carolyne Zinko & Adonis, Catherine Bigelow, Leah & Jerry Garchik. Also Hollywood's George Christy, Jeanne Lawrence (Social Diary), Jeanne (Dear Abby) Phillips, Gentry's Elsie Floriani, and the Nob Hill Gazette's Lois Lehrman.

Am grateful to my sweet husband, Lee Munson, my children Linda & Gary Zellerbach, my grandchildren Laura and Randy Zellerbach, my brother Dr. Sandor Burstein, and his wife Beth, and my niece Brooke Kettner.

Add photographers Drew Altizer, Elizabeth Armstrong, Moanalani Jeffrey, Scotty Morris, and my loyal, literate and legendary publisher Elihu Blotnick.

21 Huntington Court

PART 1

— Chapter 1 —

HE COULD SMELL a news story deaf, gagged and blindfolded. Or so his fellow journalists said, when they "roasted" him back in 1998. The occasion was the resignation of Daniel James "Cas" Casserly, who was leaving his job as Bureau Chief of the Associated Press in Washington D.C., to move to San Francisco.

Sixteen years later, in 2014, Cas Casserly had become the owner/publisher of *CityTalk*, a weekly Bay Area magazine. Time had sharpened his skills; his nose for news was keener than ever.

Perhaps that's why, for no reason at all, he'd let a bright young voice on the phone entice him to visit what was normally a pedestrian event – a block party.

"What was I thinking?" He asked himself as he searched for a shirt that Sunday morning. Peering into the mirror on his bathroom cabinet, he yawned, brushed back his dark brown hair, and reached for his horn-rimmed glasses.

Hallie Marsh, his wife, had once suggested contacts, but the idea of putting lenses in and out of his eyes appalled him.

Well aware that he was tall, dark and "uncommonly handsome," as a woman reporter once described him, Cas lacked both the time and the desire to fuss with his appearance.

Still wondering why he'd accepted a Sunday invitation, he reminded himself that he'd told the caller that he thought block parties had lost their luster, which was a lie, since he'd never given the subject the least bit of thought.

And yet, this was no ordinary block party, as it was

happening in Huntington Court, an elite cul-de-sac in the midst of the city's finest residential district. What attracted him, he realized, was the fame and accomplishments of some of the residents.

Would Vance Ferlingetty, who'd won a Pulitzer for fiction, and Anna Steinberg, who'd been a U.S. Senator for 23 years, and Lily Whang, who designed gowns that cost five figures, be likely to spend a Sunday afternoon chatting with the neighbors over beer and hot dogs?

Doubtful – but he'd promised to stop by.

— Chapter 2 —

KIMBERLY WU TAUBIN SLIPPED on her hat and dark glasses, tied a white dust mask over her nose and mouth, and bypassed the mirror as she headed for her front door.

Too bad if the neighbors thought she looked like a Martian. The hat shielded her from the sun, the glasses cut the glare, and the mask helped filter out the morning pollens.

Kim's hay fever always flared in the springtime, and Sunday, March 30th, 2014 was no exception. Despite all the antihistamines she'd gobbled, her eyes were red and itchy, her nose ran non-stop, and she knew she'd be miserable for the next two months.

The cause was no secret.

Huntington Court, sometimes called "the circle," was named for Collis Potter Huntington, a famous railroad baron of the late 1800s.

San Franciscans knew Huntington Court as a small circular enclave with a lifestyle all its own. Twenty-two impressive homes and mansions formed a ring around a central island – actually, a mini-park.

The island was the first thing visitors saw when driving through the iron gates. Luckily for Kim, the lilies, rose bushes and purple agapanthus seemed to bypass her sensitive nose.

The blossoming cherry trees, however, showed no mercy.

— Chapter 3 —

DOUBLE-LOCKING the door of 21 Huntington Court, Kim took short breaths as she hurried up the street that separated the houses from the island. Her dearest friend, Delsey de Baubery, lived at number 16, only five doors away.

Loving history as she did, Kim often thought about the origin of Huntington Court, which she'd researched before they bought their home. Long hours at the library had yielded a promotional brochure, dated 1905. It traced the property back to a French developer named Louis Hauteur, who bought a circular tract of land in San Francisco shortly before the turn of the century.

He envisioned "elegant mansions surrounding a garden of greenery," and promised that the site would harbor "no stores, saloons, or tall, ugly buildings." Wanting to separate his microcosm from the hoi polloi, he chose a local name that he thought had "a certain cachet."

Thus was born Huntington Court.

— Chapter 4 —

AND THUS BEGAN THE DAY of the Huntington Court block party Kim Taubin and Delsey de Baubery had been planning for months.

"Are the caterers here?" asked Delsey, opening her front door. "Are my jeans too tight?"

Kim slipped off her dust mask and laughed. "Not for a new divorcée." How she envied her friend's picture-perfect face and tall, curvy figure.

Petite and delicate, with iridescent skin and dainty Asian features, Kim adored her more glamorous neighbor. At 36, only a year younger than Delsey, she still called her "my big sister."

She glanced at her watch. "It's 10 o'clock, Del, so we've an hour before we start. The caterers just arrived. They're loading the barbecues and setting up the tables and jumpies for the kids. We lucked out with the weather."

Delsey brushed back a strand of long, dark hair. "Yes, it's gorgeous." A wave of wrinkles crossed her forehead. "Can you believe Ashton? He called this morning and asked if he could bring his whore! Can you imagine? I told him no, the boys aren't ready to see him with a new woman. The divorce was just final last week."

"He's a man. What do you expect?"

"You're right, they're a different species – although he did give me two fabulous sons." Delsey paused to choose her words. "Umm – are your allergies bad?"

"No worse than usual. But I hear you, and no, I won't wear my mask today. I've started a new treatment, so maybe

I won't need masks anymore."

"Shots?"

"No, sublingual drops – under the tongue. You start with a low dose of whatever you're allergic to and gradually build up immunity. It's the same principle as shots, but without the needles."

"How do the drops taste?

"Sweet. Oh – don't forget I invited that journalist, Dan Casserly, who owns *CityTalk* magazine. Sometimes they do human interest stories, and I thought he might want to cover a swanky block party. His idea, of all things, is to write about the death of the block party."

"Death?"

"Death," Kim repeated. "He said lots of people can't afford to spend money on their neighbors these days – or don't want to – so block parties are dying out. Anyway, Cas promised he'd come by to see what we were doing, and possibly send over a writer."

"Cas?"

Kim giggled. "He said that's what people call him. I told him he could bring a friend. I hope he doesn't. He sounds charming."

Delsey rolled her eyes. "If Manny sees you flirting, you're dead."

"Manny's in L.A. doing what he always does in L.A."

"Besides that?"

"It's just an overnight. He's making a commercial this morning and flying back this afternoon. Shall we check the tables?"

— Chapter 5 —

HOWARD MANVILLE "MANNY" TAUBIN was indeed in Los Angeles, and at that moment, entertaining a redhead in his hotel suite. The 6-foot-2, 260-pound former quarterback had been a high school football star when Kimberly Wu sat behind him in math class. It had taken her all of one week to be smitten by his masculine virility, his winning smile, and the fact that he completely ignored her.

Manny graduated three years ahead of Kim, played four years of college football, and went on to a starring role with the San Francisco 49ers.

An early marriage to a blonde cheerleader ended in divorce, and in 2009, he tried to ignore a torn knee ligament. He went on to sign a $20 million contract, becoming something of a legend after telling a reporter, "I play harder when it hurts because I'm trying to show that it doesn't."

At the same time, he'd often be seen around town squiring young beauties, and was memorably quoted as saying, "You're only as young as the woman you feel."

Knee injuries and two concussions finally caught up with Manny Taubin, and finishing his football career at age 34. That same year, a lovely Chinese nurse, also divorced, caught his eye in the doctor's office.

Manny had no trouble luring Kimberly Wu into his boudoir, where she proved to excel in certain physical arts. A year later, she moved into his South of Market bachelor pad, and proceeded to try to make herself indispensable.

Still working at the time, she came home one afternoon and reported that her boss, the doctor, had invited her for lunch the next day – and she'd accepted. Furious, Manny told her either to break the date or move out. She replied that she was already planning to leave, since their relationship was going nowhere.

After listening to her pull out drawers and pack suitcases for an hour, he strode into their bedroom, lifted her in his arms and set her down on the bed. "You're not going any-where, Miss Kimberly Wu," he growled. "We're getting married."

None of that was on his mind that Sunday morning, as he extracted several bills from his wallet, handed them to his guest, and opened the door to his suite. "So long," he said, "See ya next trip."

The young woman stood on tiptoes, nibbled his ear and whispered, "Bye, bye, super stud."

Then she disappeared.

— Chapter 6 —

A RAY OF BRIGHT sunlight struck Hallie Marsh's eyes as she awakened Sunday morning, then checked the clock on the wall.

"Almost nine," she mumbled, sitting up in bed. "I stayed up too late. Cas?" she called.

"Hi, honey," a voice answered. "Danny cooked breakfast. Come join us!"

"Oh, no!" Hopping out of bed, she grabbed a robe and hurried down the stairs to the kitchen. Two-year-old Danny

Casserly was sitting in his highchair banging a spoon on what looked to be a bowl of oatmeal. Seeing his mother, he grinned and pounded harder, the cereal flying everywhere.

"No, Danny, no," she said calmly, extracting the spoon from his hand, and frowning at her husband. "Whatever were you thinking, Daddy dear?"

Cas smiled guiltily. "He was just stirring his cereal like grown-ups do. Right, Danny?"

The boy looked up at his mother, turned his bowl upside down and emptied it on the floor. "All gone!" he said proudly.

— Chapter 7 —

LATE THAT AFTERNOON, having helped his wife clean the kitchen, Cas drove his family to Huntington Court. As instructed, he informed the guard at the gate that they were "guests of Ms. Taubin," then noted the sign that said, "Speed Limit 15, One Way, Private Property," and parked by the entrance.

Once Danny was secured in his stroller, the three headed for the gathering on the street. About 40 adults and children sat at tables. Fathers and sons tossed baseballs back and forth, toddlers pedaled their tricycles, and a pair of six-year-olds raced their motorized mini-cars, while pre-teeners rode their bicycles 'round and 'round. Neighbors laughed, chatted, and piled up their plates at the barbecues. The picnic spirit was high.

"And my brilliant journalist husband is writing a piece

that says block parties are dead?" asked Hallie.

"I don't know why I agreed to come here." He was starting to take notes on his iPad. "It was her voice – Kim Taubin's sweet, sensitive voice. Something about it said she had a story to tell."

Before Hallie could respond, a tall, leggy brunette came hurrying towards them. "Mr. Cassidy?"

"Close enough. This is my wife, Hallie Marsh – and our son, Danny. You must be Kim Taubin."

"No," she smiled. "We don't even look alike. I'm Delsey de Baubery and I'm so glad you could join us. Kim's been expecting you, but she's disappeared. I've been looking all over for her. It's almost three, and the party ends at four. May I introduce you to the neighbors?"

"Thanks, Delsey. Please ignore us and we'll be fine. By the way, why do you have a guard at the entrance? Is this a gated community?"

"Definitely not," she said. "The guard is just for today because all the kids are running loose. We usually have a guard on duty at night, from five to midnight, then another from midnight to seven. Some of the residents want to have guards round the clock, but Kim and I and a few others are fighting them. We don't want to close ourselves off from the city. We want people to be welcome to drive around and admire our island and our lovely homes. Next thing, the 'isolationists' will be wanting to charge admission!"

"Good for you for fighting them. Do you have these block parties often?"

"No, thank God!" She laughed. "They're more work than they're worth. But my two boys, five and seven, are having the time of their lives on that trampoline."

"Mind if I ask who pays for all this?"

"I don't mind. The Homeowners' Association rents the tables, the barbecues and the jumpies, and Kim and I pay the caterers and do everything else. Speaking of Kim, I've got to find her. She's been so looking forward to meeting you. Please take some plates and help yourselves. We've food for an army!"

— Chapter 8 —

MOMENTS LATER, Cas sat a table pecking away at his iPad. The crowd was younger than he expected and looked more like the children – or grandchildren – of the celebrities, none of whom was present. Two tables were packed with older folks and mothers with babies. The scene was hardly news.

Danny dozed peacefully in his stroller, and Hallie felt no desire to reach out to the residents, who seemed happily absorbed in themselves.

Relieved not to have to make small talk, she leaned back in her chair, thankful that she'd brought a sun hat and dark glasses. This was a rare, peaceful moment, and she was happy to let her thoughts wander.

It seemed almost a lifetime ago that she was a child, growing up minutes away from Huntington Court, in the mansion of her parents, Edith and R. Stuart Marsh. They lived on one of the three blocks of Broadway known as the "Gold Coast," or more recently, thanks to an influx of home-buyers from Silicon Valley, "Billionaire's Row."

Material wealth had never impressed Hallie. She knew that her late grandparents, Zina and Pritchard Doty, had been cattle ranchers and major landowners in Montana.

Her mother, Edith, had grown up learning how to shear sheep, fish for pike in the lake, groom horses and gallop bareback across the plains. Animals were family to her, and one day, after watching a cow give birth, she decided to become a veterinarian.

The Dotys had three daughters. Edith's two sisters married and built homes on the Montana property, but Edith had fallen in love with Bobby Marsh, an ambitious young art student she'd met at a party. When he proposed, she dropped out of veterinary school.

They wed in 1970, and moved to Berkeley, just across San Francisco Bay, where Bobby had accepted a teaching offer from the University of California.

Not long after that, Edith's parents died, leaving their assets, in equal amounts, to their three daughters. Edith sold her shares to her sisters, ending up with an unexpected bounty of $12 million.

R. Stuart Marsh – as he then wanted to be known – lost no time investing his wife's inheritance in as many French Impressionist paintings as her money would buy. They traveled across Europe, picking up art everywhere, and acquiring a formidable collection. R. Stuart's knowledge and expertise earned him a worldwide reputation as collector and connoisseur.

After his death in 1998, the sale of a single Edouard Manet allowed his widow, Edith Marsh, to become a generous benefactor of the arts.

— Chapter 9 —

GROWING UP the daughter of the wealthy Marshes, Hallie
knew that she was privileged, which sometimes made her uncomfortable. She would often invite friends to a movie,
rather than have them see the elegant manor she called home.

Years later, in 1996, fresh from Smith College with a
master's in education, Hallie came back to the city she loved
and began job hunting. At the same time, urged by her
mother, she started doing volunteer work for SFMOMA –
the San Francisco Museum of Modern Art.

To everyone's surprise, especially her own, she found she
had a knack for promoting events. Spotting her ability, a
board member recruited her to join his Public Relations
firm, headquartered in New York.

After six years in Manhattan, Hallie returned to San Francisco and opened her own PR office in the Financial District.
Edith Marsh did not approve. Her daughter didn't need to
work, and especially not in publicity, which she made a point
to shun. Hallie was constantly reminded of her mother's pet
motto: "In our family we work for a cause, not for applause."

Nevertheless, Hallie had long ago learned how to handle
her mother's domineering nature. She would simply give in,
then do whatever she pleased.

Not so her younger brother Rob, who resented "Mumsy"
– as he and his sister teasingly called her – and her constant
attempts to involve him in the art world. Defiant and frus-
trated, Rob left home. Three years later, he returned to the
city as a successful jazz guitarist, married a lovely woman,
fathered twin girls, and reunited with his family.

— Chapter 10 —

DANNY'S CRYING ended Hallie's reverie. She scolded herself for dozing, then picked up and cuddled her son.

Cas watched approvingly. "Why don't you take Danny home, honey? I'll stay till the end and see if any of the older generation show up. I should try to meet Kim, too – if I can find her."

"Okay. Caitlin will be home by now. She can feed Danny while I come back for you."

By 4:45, all the neighbors had disappeared, except for two women who were helping Delsey pack up food. The caterers and crew bustled about, folding up tables, gathering linens, utensils, and whatever else they'd brought.

Cas glanced down at his notes. Kim had told him she lived at number 21, "in a big white house, near the end of Huntington Court."

Not wanting to bother Delsey, Cas tucked his phone in his pocket and strolled up the street, easily finding his destination.

— Chapter 11 —

THINKING BACK A FEW YEARS, Cas well remembered Manny Taubin – who wouldn't? The smiling quarterback was a popular favorite, and evidently smart enough to have saved and banked most of his earnings.

Every football fan knew that quarterbacks, under intense pressure to generate points, were among the best-paid players on the team. And in those days, whenever the offense took the field, Manny Taubin would get results. After serious knee injuries and two concussions forced him to leave the game, a flood of commercial endorsements kept him paying six-figure taxes.

Cas took a moment to assess the Taubin residence. Freshly painted and modern in style, it looked as if it had been newly built, rather than remodeled. A flat roof, large glass windows, straight lines and minimal trim made it a pleasing contrast to the adjoining "gingerbread" houses. Or so Cas thought. He wondered if the neighbors agreed.

In reflection, it seemed that the block party was anything but a party. People in the circle were good at show, at pretending camaraderie for an hour or two when they'd rather be at their desks or watching a ball game.

It occurred to him that these were successful people because they'd overcome adversity, and fought hard for their victories. They believed in themselves and embraced competition. They'd won their place and were determined to show they could win on the romantic field, the financial field, on any and every field.

Perhaps they'd won so often that there was no one left to beat but the neighbors...

Rapping the brass knocker on the door, Cas heard loud clanks, but no response. He rapped again and finally rang the bell. Waiting patiently for another three minutes, he rang once more, then tried the knob. The door was unlocked!

Not sure what to do, he looked around. No one seemed

available to tell him to enter – or not to. Cautiously, he turned the handle, calling out Kim's and Manny's names. The silence concerned him.

— Chapter 12 —

STILL SHOUTING for the owners, Cas passed through the Taubins' spacious, all-white living room. It reminded him of the high-end apartments he used to visit in Washington, D.C., in the late '90s, when he was a popular "extra man," as well as heading a major wire service.

He didn't like himself much in those days. Heavy drinking, occasional coke use, and a two-year affair with Helen Kaiser, a newspaper reporter he knew he'd never marry, left him little self-respect. At Helen's urging, he joined AA, but his drinking continued, and eventually broke them up.

Subsequently, Helen moved to San Francisco, joined the police academy, graduated with honors, and worked herself up to her present position as Captain, and head of the SF Police Department's homicide detail.

Shortly after Helen's move west, Cas followed, accepting an offer to become managing editor of San Francisco's *CityTalk* magazine. But not until he met and fell in love with Hallie Marsh, a beautiful, strong-willed blonde he met on a cruise ship, did he begin to honor his AA vows.

Today, at 42, booze, drugs and wild women were only bad memories. A devoted family man, Daniel James Casserly had become the respected and powerful owner of one of the Bay Area's finest news magazines.

— Chapter 13 —

"Anybody home?" Still calling the owners, Cas wandered through the Taubins' ultra-modern dining room, noticing its white glass table and Lucite chairs that looked decidedly uncomfortable.

"I'm not a burglar!" he shouted, fairly certain that no one was listening. "Kim? Manny? Hello?"

He pushed a swinging door into the kitchen, admiring the handsome slab of black granite that served as the center counter. Beneath it, a set of drawers was neatly closed. The sink held a single dark-stained coffee mug.

Then suddenly, he gasped.

Two small feet in sandals seemed to be staring up at him. Quickly rounding the corner, he saw the rest of the woman's body. She was lying on her side with her right leg crossed over the left, as if she'd dropped to the floor unexpectedly.

"Kim!" he cried loudly, "Whoever you are! Wake up!"

The pulse on her neck was not beating. Her skin was cold. No air was coming from her mouth and no heartbeats sounded in her chest. Her face had a strange grimace. He spent five seconds snapping photos with his cell phone, then turned her slightly, and performed CPR till he was exhausted.

Finally, he shook his head and reached for his phone again. The woman – Asian, pretty, petite – had to be Kimberly Wu Taubin.

And she was dead.

PART 2

— Chapter 14 —

SOBBING SOFTLY, Delsey de Baubery stood in a corner of the kitchen, staring down at her lifeless friend. Sirens sounded just as Cas took her arm and suggested they meet the officers at the front door.

A police car and an ambulance pulled up at the same time. Paramedics dashed in and followed Cas to the kitchen. They confirmed the woman's death and questioned Cas. Yes, he'd found her and hadn't gotten a pulse. Yes, he'd taken quick pictures of the body and the surroundings before he started cardiopulmonary resuscitation. Yes, he'd been trained and certified as a lifeguard.

A plain-clothed photographer snapped shots of the kitchen, the dead woman, and everything else in the vicinity, while two uniformed police looked over the scene.

Delsey told them what she knew. She'd been with Kim Taubin most of the morning getting ready for the block party. About 11 a.m., Kim said she'd be right back and that was the last time anyone saw her.

After calling Hallie with the sad news, Cas explained his presence to the police, who thanked him for taking pictures and confiscated his phone. Then he heard one of the officers' speak into his headset: "Chinese-American woman, age 36, reportedly in good health. No sign of foul play or forced entrance, no blood, no witnesses. Body cold. Get crime scene and M.E. here ASAP!"

— Chapter 15 —

HALLIE DROVE UP to the house just as her friendly nemesis, veteran homicide inspector Sergeant Theodore "TB" Baer, and his partner, Officer Lenny Brisco arrived, along with the M.E., Chief Medical Examiner Dr. Thomas Toy.

TB scowled. "Dammit, Hallie Marsh, what are you doing here?"

"Nice of you to ask, TB." She smiled. "My husband found the poor woman's body."

"You don't say. Did he kill her?"

"That's not funny."

Despite the dozen or so cases she had helped him solve over the years, TB hadn't curtailed his sarcasm. And it still annoyed her. Cas said the detective needed to get laid. Whenever men had a problem, Hallie noted, other men assumed they needed sex.

Her own diagnosis blamed the male ego. What self-respecting homicide cop would want to have an amateur find clues he'd missed? And a female at that!

Lenny had once told her that his husky 6-foot-6-inch partner had turned down a lucrative basketball contract. TB liked to say that he'd gone for the badge instead of the basket. Too bad, Hallie thought. His competitive, bullying nature might have served him well in sports.

And yet, according to his supervisor, Captain Helen Kaiser, TB was the most brilliant detective on the force – as hard and as tough as he appeared. How well Hallie knew that shock of unruly gray hair, the reddish complexion, the flattened nose that made him look like a prizefighter, the gruff voice and manner.

His smile and teasing tone hadn't fooled her the first time they met, and they didn't fool her now. Neither did his firm, oh-so-sincere handshake.

But his eyes told the truth. They gave him away. They were like steel icepicks that poked right through to your brain.

— Chapter 16 —

A DECADE YOUNGER at 45, Lenny Brisco was an obvious contrast to his cool partner. Outgoing and impulsive, Lenny was a people-person, open and friendly by nature, yet hard-hitting when he had to be. A receding hairline did little to enhance his bland features, but his body was firm and muscular, and his enthusiasm contagious. Women seemed drawn to him.

Those close to Lenny also knew that he thought Hallie Marsh was one of the smartest, loveliest women he'd ever met. TB's jabs disturbed him, but he knew better than to intervene. A wink or a smile from Hallie would reassure him that she considered the source – and wasn't offended.

Their interchange, however, did not go unnoticed. TB would later remind Lenny that both he and Hallie wore wedding rings.

Lenny's answer was always the same: "Marriage doesn't mean you can't admire beautiful women. Most of the time I just pretend to flirt. Acting's in my blood."

And he believed it was. In spare moments, Lenny would often relive his starring roles in high school plays. Theatre was his passion, and in younger days, he'd hoped for a movie or TV career.

After four years of rejections and failed auditions, however, he changed course, took his policeman father's advice and joined the force. When tempted to look back with regrets, he'd remind himself of the times he'd survived on day-old bread and a can of beans.

At the station, the two partners were admired for their good-cop/bad-cop routine with suspects. Deliberately switching personalities, good guy Lenny would take the lead as the heartless prosecutor, while TB would pretend to defend the person. Known to be merciless interrogators, the pair had a record number of confessions.

— Chapter 17 —

WEARING DARK-COLORED suits and loosened ties, the two detectives and Dr. Toy, the Medical Examiner, hurried to the kitchen, where Delsey, Cas, the police and the paramedics had gathered. The photographer was checking the rooms upstairs.

"Hope no one's touched the body," growled TB.

"I was trying to save her life," said Cas.

Before TB could answer, Dr. Toy kneeled on the floor and began his preliminary inspection. "Possible bruising from CPR," he mumbled.

TB frowned. "TOD?"

"Body temp puts Time of Death between 11:30 a.m. and 1:00 p.m. today. Rigor appears to have started at approximately 3:00 p.m."

"How can you tell?" asked Cas, taking mental notes. What a scoop he'd have if he owned a daily newspaper instead of a weekly magazine.

Dr. Toy looked up in surprise. He wasn't used to being asked for explanations.

"Get on with the inspection!" urged TB.

"Mr. Casserly deserves an answer, Detective." Dr. Toy continued quietly. "Rigor Mortis sets in because the body loses its ATP – Adenosine Triphosphate – the substance which controls the muscles. The jaw and upper extremities contract, causing the somewhat smirking expression you see on the decedent's face."

"Thanks," said Cas. "Sorry to have disturbed you."

"These chemical changes in the muscles," the M.E. continued, ignoring TB's scowl, "cause the corpse to stiffen and be difficult to manipulate. Full Rigor sets in 9 to 12 hours after death."

"That's why dead bodies are called 'stiffs,' " said Lenny.

"Shut up, Brisco!" TB frowned. "The sooner we know the facts, the sooner we can start looking for whoever did this."

Dr. Toy's calm voice broke the heavy silence that followed. "To continue," he went on, "I find no evidence of homicide at this early date. That does not rule it out."

He shone a flashlight into the victim's mouth. "Slight glossitis – swelling of the tongue and throat. Bluish pigmentation of skin, no defense wounds, no signs of physical trauma. I'll know more when I get the body on the table. Could be poison. Possibly self-administered."

"No way!" cried Delsey. "Kim was so happy this morning. Her husband's coming back from L.A. tonight – " She stopped suddenly. "Omigod, she was going to meet him at the airport!"

"What time?" asked TB.

"She didn't say. But he's sure to call when she doesn't show up. Did you find her cell?"

"Yeah, it's right here." One of the policemen set an iPhone and a Vuitton bag on the counter. "And there's a reporter out front taking pix of the house."

"Damn!" Lenny pursed his lips. "I told that guard no one comes in but residents and cops."

"There's another entrance on River Street," said Delsey. "The gate's locked, but someone could've hopped over it."

"Then seal the damn thing off!" Lenny's hands flew up in the air. "And for God's sake, officers, get more backup. This is gonna be one big fat headache when the news breaks."

— Chapter 18 —

MOMENTS LATER, Lenny grabbed Kim Taubin's ringing phone. "We need a woman's voice so Manny won't think it's the wrong number and hang up." He thrust the mobile at Hallie, who quickly passed it to Delsey.

"Oh, shit," she whispered, pausing to collect herself. "I'll put him on speakerphone. Er – Hello?"

"Where the hell are you?" said an angry voice. "You

31

sound funny."

"Hi, Manny. It's Delsey. Umm – Kim won't be able to pick you up. Can you grab a cab?"

"Where the hell is she? What's wrong?"

"She's had an accident –"

"Is she okay?"

"Uh…" TB grabbed the phone. "Mr. Taubin? This is Officer Theodore Baer speaking. We can't give you any information right now. If you tell me your location, I'll send a police car for you."

"Fuck the damn police car! Where's my wife?"

Delsey took back the phone. "Just get your ass home, Manny," she said and clicked off.

Thirty minutes passed. Two police cars waited at the gates. When Manny's cab pulled up, TB hurried over, took the passenger's suitcase, and broke the news to him as gently as he could. Manny was silent with shock as they walked the short distance to his home. Yellow tape already surrounded the area; police were holding back a crowd of curious neighbors.

Drained and pale, Manny hurried into his living room where his wife's covered body lay on a gurney. He lifted the sheet, stared a moment, then quietly began to cry. Delsey came running over and embraced him – as they sobbed in each other's arms.

PART 3

— Chapter 19 —

ZELDA RHINEHART lived four doors over, at 17 Huntington Court. She was among the onlookers when Hallie and Cas came out the front door of the Taubin house, ducked under the yellow tape and ran to their car. Hearing her name called, Hallie turned, waved, then climbed into the front seat. They drove off quickly.

"Who was that?" asked Cas.

"A nosey neighbor I see at gym," said Hallie. "I'm sure she wants to know what's going on, and TB made me promise not to talk to anyone till the story breaks."

"That would be…right now." Cas steered with one hand; the other dialed his wife's phone. A voice boomed over the car's speaker: "Newsroom. What's up, Cas?"

"Got a short one for you, Maggie. Ready?"

"Shoot!"

"At approximately 5:15 this afternoon, police answered a call to – what's that address, Hal'?"

"21 Huntington Court."

"Got it," said Maggie.

Cas continued, "…where they found the body of 36-year-old Kimberly Wu Taubin on the kitchen floor. TOD estimated between 11:30 a.m. and 1:00 p.m."

"Manny's wife?"

"Yup. No sign of forced entrance or foul play. The cops and the M.E. are there now."

"Where's Manny?"

"He just drove in from the airport. When we left, he and their neighbor Delsey somebody –"

"De Baubery," said Hallie.

"They were hugging and crying over the body...that's all I have for you, Mag."

"Thanks, Cas. I'm streaming it as we speak."

"Was that KCIT-TV?" asked Hallie, seconds later.

"Yup. It'll be old news by the time *CityTalk* gets out, so I figured I'd make a few points with Maggie. She'll be grateful for the scoop."

"Grateful! Doesn't anyone do things anymore just to be nice? It seems every good deed we do is about payback."

Cas laughed. "Right on, sweetheart. Welcome to 2014."

— **Chapter 20** —

MONDAY morning's *Chronicle* blared: MANNY TAUBIN'S WIFE FOUND DEAD." The sub-head read, "Mystery Stumps Police," and the story reported the few facts they had. Cas was mentioned as having found the body, and Delsey's picture showed her wiping her eyes while talking to TB.

Tuesday's paper followed up. Manny refused to speak to the press, which inspired reporters to pounce on the mystery factor and capture the public's interest. Manny was offering a $10,000 reward for info leading to capture and conviction, as well as asking for help from anyone who knew anything. Initial word from the M.E. was that the death could have been accidental.

A day passed. Wednesday afternoon, Lenny was pleased to

have an excuse to phone Hallie. She answered promptly.

"It's Lenny Brisco," he said. "You know – TB's partner?"

"Hi, Lenny. Any news?"

"That's why I'm calling. That Manny Taubin is one stubborn guy – didn't want his wife's body cut up. We finally convinced him that he'd never know how she died without an autopsy."

"Has Dr. Toy made a prelim?"

"Yeah, but it's inconclusive. Post-mortem findings indicate COD – Cause of Death as yet unknown. Let's see – here it is: 'Slight laryngeal edema, eosinophilia in lungs, heart and tissues, evidence of myocardial hypoperfusion' and lots more jibberish I can't pronounce. I'm told it means a swollen tongue and not enough blood flow to the heart."

"Lividity?"

"Confirms Toy's findings."

"Toxins?

"Nothing yet. We'll get the tox screen and blood cultures in six weeks. Toy found no evidence of illness, disease, or foul play. Apparently death came fast and she didn't suffer. She did have some facial scratches. He thinks they were self-administered."

"That doesn't make sense," said Hallie frowning. Her friend Delsey said she was happy and not the least bit depressed. Did Kim have a cat?"

"Nope, no pets. Oh, yeah. TB said I could report this to you, but he asked me to tell you to keep your pretty nose out of this."

"I doubt he said 'pretty,' Lenny. Tell him it's a free country."

THAT EVENING, a uniformed guard crossed his hands in the air as Hallie pulled up to the gates of Huntington Court. "This crime scene," he announced. "Nobody come in."

She rolled down her window and peeked out. "You must be Dmitri. I'm visiting Ms. de Baubery in number 16. She said she'd tell you I was coming."

"Ah, Miss Delsey!" He broke into a grin. "Okay, Miss Delsey call me. Go in, go in."

"Thank you."

How different Huntington Court looked at night, Hallie thought, as she drove through the gate. Despite the bright street lights; house numbers were barely visible. No one was out walking, no cars drove by, no children played in the street. The silence was almost eerie.

Fortunately, Delsey had told her to look for a green porch light, and there was only one. Marveling at the number of empty parking spaces – a rare sight in San Francisco – Hallie stopped in front of a sprawling red brick mansion. Well-manicured shrubbery and a pair of marble columns framed the entrance.

"Classic," Hallie said to herself, "and somewhat forbidding." No surprise. The homeowner had not been friendly when they met at the Taubin house, but what did she expect? Delsey had just lost her best friend.

Yet Delsey had been quite pleasant on the phone when Hallie mentioned that her mother was Edith Marsh, and they had met at her stepmother Babe de Baubery's Christmas party. After that, Delsey hadn't hesitated when Hallie asked if she could drop by for a chat.

— Chapter 22 —

TALL AND ELEGANT in a pink satin at-home gown, Delsey de Baubery answered her front door. Hallie regarded her in surprise. What a difference from the frantic young woman in T-shirt and jeans who'd screamed at Manny Taubin to move his ass!

Curls of long, dark hair rested on her shoulders. Devoid of makeup, her eyes seemed larger than remembered, giving her face a youthful innocence. An unexpected embrace canceled Hallie's first impression. Her host was neither cold nor unfriendly.

"Now I remember meeting you and your mother at my stepmother's," Delsey said, smiling. "I thought how lovely you are and wondered if you were married. My brother's getting a divorce."

Hallie laughed. "I'm very married, but thanks for the compliment. Didn't I read that you —"

"Yes, I just got divorced, too. Runs in the family, I guess." She took Hallie's arm as they walked into the living room. "Babe, my wicked stepmother, is very fond of your mother. She said she was fond of you, too, but couldn't remember your name. Won't you sit down? Would you like a drink or some tea?"

"Nothing, thanks." Hallie glanced around the room and settled on a couch. "Your home is so elegant. I'm more into modern, but I appreciate beautiful antiques." After a few seconds, she asked, "Is Babe really a wicked stepmother?"

Delsey dropped into an armchair and carefully crossed her legs. "I'm sure you know the story. Everyone does. Daddy saw the picture of Miss Beatrice Brown modeling lingerie in the Victoria's Secret catalogue, and got hot pants. They started dating, she held him off, held out for marriage, and guess what! Behold the Countess Babe de Baubery! I have to give her credit for pushing herself to the top of the social A-list. But as a kind, caring person, she might as well fly off on her broom."

"That's too bad."

"She won't ever talk about her family or where she grew up. I've a hunch her dear old dad used to get into her jammies. But you didn't come here to discuss Babe."

"You're right," said Hallie. "I'm terribly sorry about Kim. I know you two were close."

"Like sisters." Delsey's eyes began to tear. "That policeman, Lenny, said you're some kind of amateur sleuth. Is that why you're here?"

"In a way. I love puzzles – all kinds. And I also know that the two homicide detectives investigating Kim's death have more cases than they can handle right now. I'm afraid they might take the easy road, accept her death as accidental, and close the file. Entre nous?"

"Absolutely."

"I go on instinct a lot. Sometimes I'm wrong but more often I'm right. And I have the strongest feeling that there's more to Kim's death than some kind of accident. It's too neat, too easy. When the M.E.'s report –"

"M.E.?"

"Medical Examiner. The coroner. When his autopsy's done and the tox screen for poisons and other tests come back in six weeks, we'll know a lot more. For now, we've no choice but to be patient."

— Chapter 23 —

DELSEY DABBED at her eyes with a lace hankie. "Will we truly know more, Hallie? My dear friend was young, bright, happy with her life, and to the best of our knowledge, in excellent health. Yet you're afraid the police are so busy, they'll call her death accidental and sweep it under the rug?"

"They won't do anything illegal or unethical, but if they accept the coroner's first ruling that the death could be accidental, they might not look any farther. And without their recommendation, the coroner – who also has a huge backlog of cases and the public screaming about delays – will probably close the file."

"Wouldn't that be better for everyone?"

"And let a possible killer go free? Don't you want justice for Kim? What about closure for Manny and her family?"

"I want that, certainly."

"Can you think of anyone who'd want to hurt her? Has anyone ever threatened her?

"Good Lord, no! Everyone – well, most everyone – loved Kimmie. And she loved Huntington Court – except for the cherry blossom trees. Every spring, especially when we have the Cherry Blossom Festival, she'd get terrible allergies. She's been trying for years to replace the trees at her own cost, but the residents won't hear of it. They say tourists call us 'Cherry Blossom Circle,' and come from all over the world to see our trees in bloom."

"Is that true?"

"Actually it is. We have pictures of the trees on postcards. They're our logo on our website. They're even on the car stickers that identify us as residents. The homeowners say that if we were to lose the cherry trees, our property values would drop."

"Which homeowners?"

"Quite a few. They say – well, they said that Kim could afford to get out of town for two months every year, the creeps. Kim did so much good for us. She was even writing a book for the residents. History was her passion, and she spent days doing research. Each home has its own architect, its own story, its own picture, professionally photographed by Scotty Drew. This was going to be a stunning coffee table book."

"Were you helping her?"

"It was Kim's project, but yes, I'm pretty good at grammar and spelling, and I edited her writing. Together, we interviewed 16 of the 22 families. Not counting Manny and me, we have four families to go, but either they weren't available, or they declined to be interviewed. Despite that, the other neighbors have asked me to finish the book."

"Will you?"

Delsey's face fell. "I wish I could. But honestly…I'm not a writer."

Chapter 24

HALLIE CHECKED her watch and stood up to leave. "Neither am I, Delsey. But I spent 12 years running a Public Relations firm, interviewing clients and writing brochures. Perhaps I could help."

"You mean it? That would be fabulous! All we need are six interviews: one with Manny, one with me, and four with the jerks who weren't available. Then the first draft will be ready for the publisher. We were lucky to sign with Allen House. They do magnificent art books."

"I'd be happy to interview you, and I could Google Manny for information, and then try to reach the holdouts. Will you send me their names? And the first draft? I'm anxious to read about all the residents."

Delsey looked confused for a few seconds. Then she stared in disbelief. "You think someone in Huntington Court might have killed Kim?"

"It's a good place to start. Obviously, the neighbors have strong feelings about guards and property values and cherry blossom trees."

"But you're not a resident. How would I explain you?"

"Tell the truth. You asked a friend to help you finish the book. And if they've heard that I like to solve mysteries, all the better."

"Oh Lordy, what to do." Delsey clasped her hands. "The police took Kim's computer. I don't know what kind of terrorist plots they expect to find on it. Luckily, though, Kim kept me up to date so I can send you the draft. The book would be a wonderful memorial to her. But – forgive my asking – why would you want to do this?"

Hallie paused before answering. Then she said, "It's quite simple, Delsey. I'd like to know why an innocent young woman with everything to live for, suddenly dies. Corny as it sounds, I want to see justice for Kim as much as you do. My hunches are strong, and unfortunately, they're usually right. I just pray that this time…I'm wrong."

— Chapter 25 —

A WEEK PASSED with no word from Delsey and no calls for help from the police. Not that Hallie expected them. Lenny did send an email stating that the M.E. had "finished cutting up the body," and promised to inform her when they get the final autopsy report.

The press continued to track the investigation, despite the public's growing indifference. While sport fans felt sorry for their hero, Manny, other readers were quick to point out that a wealthy Asian woman, who may have died of natural causes, was getting far more attention than gunshot victims in poorer parts of town. The police responded, and began to turn their efforts elsewhere.

About the same time, Delsey called Hallie. She apologized for taking so long to proof-check the copy, but now it was ready for the final touches. She also had two tickets to an American Conservatory Theater matinee the next day, and could Hallie join her? They could get a bite afterwards and discuss the book.

Cas was in Los Angeles attending a convention and Hallie

was delighted to accept.

— Chapter 26 —

"THE PLAY was terrific, but I'm wondering if it's too soon for me to be seen in public." Delsey glanced around nervously as she and Hallie slipped into a booth at Mel's Drive-In. It wasn't a real drive-in, just one of the few restaurants in town where you could still get a thick milkshake in a metal tumbler.

"Nonsense." Hallie handed her a menu. "Nobody's expecting you to act like a widow. Sitting home mourning doesn't help Kim. Did you bring me the draft?"

"Yes, I have the CD in my purse. The finished book should be about 80 pages. The text will give you a better idea what kind of people live in Huntington Court. Everyone thinks we're so snobby."

"Aren't you?"

"No, not most of us," said Delsey. "I admit we're not blue collar. We're more white collar with Hermès ties. We live in multi-million dollar homes, and we work hard at whatever we do. Right now, I'm chairing a fundraiser for Compassion & Choices – death with dignity. My mother suffered terribly at the end of her life, and it was so unnecessary. What I mean, I guess, is that most of us don't have the time or patience to sweat the petty stuff that goes on in Huntington Court. I'm about to resign from the board."

She stopped to order a hamburger rare. Hallie chose a tuna on rye and a chocolate shake.

"Look at it this way," Delsey continued. "My neighbors have made or inherited enough money to live in an expensive area. Many of them could afford to marry the man or woman of their dreams, and they're generally happy. As I said, they work hard – if not for others, for themselves. The American ethic is to make barrels of money and then more money, isn't it?"

"It's also 'love thy neighbor.' Apparently, you have feuds and arguments like everyone else."

"Oh, sure, number 12's dog peed on number 13's lawn, and the people at 13 gave the dog a laxative and almost killed him. One family's teen-age son let the air out of their neighbors' tires because the neighbors parked too near their driveway. There's enough squabbling, small-mindedness, and piss-ant one-upmanship to go around – and then some!"

— Chapter 27 —

"AT THE SAME TIME," Delsey went on, "we're still a class act. We're not a housing development in suburbia. We don't have luaus where the women prance around in coconut bras and grass skirts, and the men wear Hawaiian shirts and make jokes about leis. I know, I once went to a country luau. They all got bombed, then it was grab and grope time. Ashton Crocklebank led the grope charge."

The waiter set down a milkshake and an iced tea.

"Your ex?"

"Very ex." She peeled the paper off a straw and stirred her drink. "Ours was an arranged marriage. Our parents were buddies. My dad and my step-mom Babe plotted and schemed with the Crocklebanks for years. They'd buy tickets for events – Opera, Symphony, theater, and each couple would get three tickets instead of two, so Ashton and I could go along. We got to know each other as teenagers, and we were good friends."

"What happened?"

"We grew up. I had no interest in dating him, but he was horny and liked my body, and my parents kept pushing me to go out with him. The next thing I knew we were engaged. I won't bore you with details, but let's just say he broke the marriage vows – on our honeymoon."

"Oh, no!"

"Now it's your turn to talk." Delsey poured catsup on her hamburger. "This looks yummy."

"I can tell you my story in a few sentences," said Hallie. "I had a double mastectomy at age 32. The cancer was 'in situ' – contained. They removed one breast, got it all, then took the other as a precaution. I was devastated, and I was sure no man would ever want me. Mumsy – my Mom – decided I needed cheering, and sent me and a girlfriend on a cruise. Cas was on board. He kept trying to flirt and I kept rejecting him. When I finally told him about my surgery, he said, 'So what? I'm an ex-alcoholic.' That changed everything."

"He's sinfully handsome," said Delsey. "Even in my state of shock, I thought, 'What a hunk!' "

"And he's as sweet and thoughtful as he is hunky." Hallie reached into her purse for a tape recorder. "Hope you don't mind, but may I interview you?"

PART 4

— Chapter 28 —

A LOUD MALE VOICE leaving a message on the answering machine awoke Hallie two mornings later. "Miss Marsh? Manny Taubin here. Sorry I never thanked your husband for tryin' so hard to save my wife. Delsey tells me you're helpin' her finish the book. That's nice of you. I'm callin' to invite you both to a celebration of Kimberly's life. Just a few friends here at the house at four tomorrow. Please call Kim's sister Jessica Wu Fong. She's stayin' at the Fairmont." Click.

"Doesn't the shmuck know it's Sunday?" Cas groaned to his wife, as the bedroom door swung open.

"Mama! Dada!" cried a joyful Danny, dashing toward the bed.

"Dear me, I'm so sorry!" The nanny tried vainly to restrain her charge. "Danny heard the phone ring and assumed you were awake."

"That's okay, Caitlin." Hallie smiled. "It's time to get dressed, anyway."

Cas picked up his giggling son and held him in the air. "If you weren't so damn cute," he whispered, "Your Mommy and I might've made you a little sister."

Jessica Wu Fong sounded friendly a few hours later, when she answered the phone.

Hallie introduced herself. "I'm calling to tell you my husband and I will be at the Memorial tomorrow. I'm terribly sorry for your loss. May we bring something? Cookies? Wine?"

48

"No, thanks. Manny hired Kim's favorite caterer. Did you know my sister well?"

"I never had the pleasure of meeting her. She invited my husband to the block party. He publishes a news magazine, and she had some sort of story in mind. Are you her only sibling?"

"Yes, I'm three years older. Our parents died last year in a car crash. So this is – I still can't believe she's gone."

"My deepest condolences. I won't keep you. Please let me know if there's anything I can do."

"Just look after Manny, if you would. He's going to need his friends."

— Chapter 29 —

LATER THAT DAY, Hallie sat staring at her computer. The iPad was great for working away from home, but for serious matters that called for concentration, she preferred the large screen and keyboard.

To her surprise, Kim's book was well written and carefully researched. The photos of the 22 homes were superb, and their histories fascinating. Kim had kept the personal paragraphs short, letting the pictures tell the story.

Efforts to contact the last four residents by phone had failed, frustrating Kim, and somewhat angering her. Reading Kim's notes, Hallie could understand that Senator Anna Steinberg, who spent most of her time in D.C., was unavailable for an interview, designer Lily Whang was almost always in New York, and she'd heard that Pulitzer Prize winner Vance Ferlingetty was seriously ill, none of which mattered since Kim had written their bios from Google. The other four neighbors, however, had given various excuses.

Kim had left their pages blank opposite pictures of their homes, except for a few notations:

> *Sharon Sampson & Charlotte McKeen; married gay couple, warm, charming, but, "We like our privacy."
> *Dr. Harvey "Rube" Rubin, widower, oncologist; off to visit friends in Hawaii. "Try me when I'm back, in a week or so." Patch on left eye.
> *Bart Willroch, married to social butterfly Christina; banker, bigot, asshole, anti-Semite. Calls the enclave "Circumcision Circle." Rumored to be shtupping Melanie (see below).
> *Efrem Bronstyn (paints nudes) & bitchy wife Melanie (interior designer) "Sorry, no time for interviews." Big scar on face.

Whose face, his or hers? Hallie wondered. It seemed obvious that three of the families had little interest in Kim's project, and that contacting them would be futile. She would, however, try to reach the doctor.

— Chapter 30 —

FORTY-ONE GUESTS met at Manny Taubin's home for what the hastily-printed program called, "Celebration of Life Ceremony – a Memorial to our Beloved Kimberly."

50

Hallie and Cas were among the last to arrive, shortly before four. A young Asian-American man in a dark suit showed them to a seat in the living room.

The hosts had set up six rows of chairs facing a makeshift podium with a lectern. Behind it, Delsey de Baubery stood tall and unsmiling. Her brownish-black hair was bobbed short and combed back behind her ears, framing an oval-shaped face. Her skin glowed, her eyes spoke of sadness.

The black Chanel pantsuit she wore, Hallie noted, made Delsey look more like a fashion ad than a woman in mourning. Her outfit was free of jewelry save for a small diamond heart pin.

"She cleans up well," whispered Cas, trying to downplay the attraction he felt. The fitted T-shirt and skintight jeans she'd worn at the block party had not escaped his notice.

Hallie nodded. She sensed her husband's admiration, but her mind was elsewhere. Gazing about, she remembered that the room was starkly white and devoid of clutter the day Cas found Kim's body.

For the ceremony, however, Kim's friends and relatives had filled every bare surface with vases of roses, and papered the walls with poster-size pictures of Kim, mostly with Manny.

The service was short. William Slide, retired Bishop of the Episcopal Church of California, spoke briefly and affectionately, adding a gentle plug for his nonprofit, and his dream to unite world religions.

Kim was not a church-goer, but Manny and the Bishop were golf buddies, and the two couples had been close.

Jessica Wu Fong, Kim's sister, and Dr. Andrew Bradstreet, Kim's former employer, delivered praise-filled speeches. Delsey spoke of her friend's charitable works and accomplishments, and managed to squeeze in a mention of Kim's well-researched book about Huntington Court homes.

"You'll be pleased to learn that my good friend Hallie Marsh has offered to finish it for publication," she said. "It's full of historical facts and flattering photos of each home. I know you'll all be as delighted as I am with the end product."

The Bishop closed the program: "Blessed be the name of the Lord," he said, raising his hands. "Amen."

Cas took his wife's arm. "Amen," he whispered. "Can we go now?"

"Soon, sweetheart," she answered. "I need a few minutes to mingle."

— Chapter 31 —

DELSEY LED the way into the dining room. A crowded table offered several kinds of sushi, meatballs, giant prawns, and salmon and cream cheese on mini-bagels A nearby buffet held trays of fruit on skewers, pastries, and a bowl of blue M&M's with Kim's picture on each candy.

Grateful that Delsey had heeded her request to have name tags, Hallie left her husband at the food spread, and headed for the man whose badge read: "Andy Bradstreet."

"What a caring talk you gave, Dr. Bradstreet," she said, introducing herself. "If I didn't know better, I'd think you were in love with Kim."

"Everyone was in love with Kim." He smiled. "She worked for me for six years and never had anything negative to say. I mean – she was human, and some of my patients were difficult, but I never saw her be rude or lose her cool. When she told me she was leaving me to marry Manny, I felt as if she'd stabbed me. I knew he wasn't the man for her, but love is strange and here they've lasted three years, so it couldn't have all been bad."

"Ummm, no," Hallie said, hiding her shock that he would speak so frankly to a stranger, "You obviously felt close to Kim. Was Manny aware of your feelings?"

The doctor scratched the back of his head. He stood about five-foot-six, with an overworked-scientist slump, a receding hairline and a concerned expression.

"I've never met Manny and I talk too much, Ms. Marsh. Is that handsome man pigging out over there your husband?"

She laughed. "Yes. He knows I hate to cook and he'd better eat dinner while he can."

"Lucky man. Nice meeting you."

Turning abruptly, the doctor hurried across the room.

— **Chapter 32** —

DOCTORS were not always proficient in the social graces, Hallie reminded herself as she looked around for Cas. She knew that some physicians studied and worked so hard, they had little time for a social life, or even to read a newspaper.

But you didn't consult a doctor to hear the latest news or gossip, and if he or she focused on patients to the exclusion of almost everything else, he or she was probably the kind of doctor you wanted.

A tall, husky man with shoulder-length gray curls and a deep scar from cheek to chin, caught her eye. His name immediately came to mind: Efrem Bronstyn, one of the people who had declined to be interviewed.

She approached him cautiously. "Mr. Bronstyn?"

He spun around, "My, what a pretty lady. You are —?"

"Hallie Marsh." She extended her hand, which he promptly kissed.

"Enchanted, my dear. You were a friend of the deceased? I wasn't too fond of Kimberly, but I saw her at neighborhood meetings and found her exceedingly attractive. Once I asked if I could paint her. She said yes, but she refused to model in the nude."

Hallie took a few seconds to respond. Who were these strange people who couldn't wait to spill their intimate secrets? "You're a painter, Mr. Bronstyn?"

"An artist, my dear. I paint, and I do sculptures, too. I'm just finishing my six-foot marble resin statue of the Greek goddess Cleopatra…in all her natural glory."

"What's marble resin?"

"It's an elastomer-based thermo plastic urethane compound – that is, a plastic that looks like marble. I'm planning to plant Cleo right-smack on our front lawn. The neighbors will have kittens."

He chuckled, drew out a card and handed it to her. "For your information, I'm quite a well-known artist. And not a struggling one. My works grace the walls of some of the most impressive collectors in the country."

"Do you paint and sculpt anything besides nude women?"

"I've a New York gallery show running as we speak. The reviews have been excellent. The paintings are my interpretations of famous entertainers who have passed on: Liz Taylor, Marilyn Monroe, Rita Hayworth, Cary Grant – and yes, they're naked as the day they were born. People are so ridiculously puritanical about genitalia. A man's penis says a lot about the man, don't you agree?"

His bait was too obvious. "Why don't you ask your wife? Is she here?"

"Oh, good Lord, no! Melanie and Kim hated each other. And frankly, m'dear, Kim's effect on Melanie was almost lethal to our marriage. You see, Melanie's an interior designer and flowers are her passion. She hires the landscape architect who cares for the island. Kim was always battering Melanie to get rid of the blossom trees which she thought caused her allergies."

"Understandable."

"No, it was pure speculation, and got Melanie extremely upset. She adores the cherry blossoms. They're beautiful beyond words. Besides, they're the symbol of Huntington Court, and she wouldn't think of destroying them."

"I see."

"The last time Kim started bitching about her allergies, Melanie told her to shut up and take a pill. I thought they were coming to blows."

He paused a few seconds, then quickly added, "I trust that this book of Kim's you're working on does not delve into personal matters?"

Hallie took note. Not everyone loved Kim. Could Melanie have a motive for murder? "I'm sure you'll be pleased with the book," she said. "It's purely historical. Just for my own curiosity, if Kim and your wife didn't get along, why did you come today?"

"A simple neighborly gesture."

"And that's why your wife's not here?"

"Would you go to a Memorial Service for someone you hated?"

"No. And I wouldn't send my husband, either. Excuse me, Mr. Bronstyn, nice to meet you."

— Chapter 33 —

Cas had apparently satisfied his hunger and was able to catch Hallie's eye in time to give her the "Let's go home" look. She raised her index finger meaning "Not just yet." Nodding reluctantly, he returned to the table. Meeting strangers and making small talk were not his strong points.

"You should try one of these," said a female voice he didn't recognize.

He turned to face a plump older woman hovering over a tray of cookies. "I'm Zelda Rhinehart," she said, "I know your wife from gym. You must be Mr. Casserly."

"So I am," he said, forcing a smile. "How do you do?"

"I do fine. Don't tell Hallie you saw me eating brownies. You're the one who found Kim's body?"

"Uh – Yes." His tone said: "Don't bother me. Go away."

"What a shame. I told Kim she shouldn't be snooping

around and digging up the neighbors' secrets. God only knows what she put in that book of hers. My two sons are in prison for some stupid drug conviction. I told Kim that if she wrote one word about them, I'd come after her with my husband's shotgun. Too bad she's dead, but I'm horrified to hear that your wife is finishing that awful book."

Cas perked up. "I think you'll find that it's historical, not personal. Why did you tell Kim about your sons if you didn't want her to know?"

"Kim and I were friends. We trusted each other. Before she started that dreadful project, we used to take walks around the circle. I knew about her fights with Melanie and the other cherry blossom nuts, and she knew about my problems with my boys. I never expected she'd put my secrets in writing."

"Are you sure she did?"

"I'm just guessing. She was such a nosey little thing. I wouldn't be surprised if one of the neighbors snuck arsenic in her corn flakes."

"You don't think her death was accidental?"

"Not for a minute. There were too many neighbors who felt threatened when they found out she was writing a book about them. I can't believe anyone I know would actually kill someone, but I have to admit her death is a relief to all of us."

"It looks like the book's going to be printed, anyway."

"Who knows? Well, nice talking with you, Mr. Casserly. Tell Hallie I'll sue her to high heaven if she writes anything about my boys. Now I'm going to pay my respects to poor Manny and go home."

PART 5

— Chapter 34 —

"OHMIGOD!" Hallie climbed into their car while Cas closed her door. "I saw you got stuck talking to Zelda. What did she have to say?"

Cas started the motor. "Nothing important – just that she thinks someone slipped arsenic into Kim's corn flakes. Oh yes, and she'll sue you to high heaven if you mention that her sons are in prison."

"Why would I do that? Did you tell her the book is mainly historical?"

"Yes, but she wasn't listening. Suggest you tell her yourself when you see her at your gym. I just wanted to escape."

Patiently, he reported the rest of their conversation, adding, "I'm not supposed to tell you that she ate a brownie."

"She has a weight problem, poor thing, along with a vivid imagination and a touch of paranoia. Sometimes I wish I were a real writer to chronicle all these characters. But who'd believe the truth about this place? Here's one of the most outstanding sections of the city. The residents have fantastic homes and all the luxuries money can buy. They're the luckiest people on the planet, and what do they do? They quibble about cherry blossom trees!"

"So I hear."

"Delsey's on the homeowners' board at the moment. She's their secretary so she has to take notes and write up their nonsense. She said some of them fight about every little thing: whether to have daytime guards or just at night. Some want to make it a 'gated community' and keep out strangers. They argue about homeowners' dues – monthly or quarterly?

They complain about neighbors parking near their driveways. They quarrel about how much to give the gardener at Christmas. It's incredible!"

Cas frowned. "Then why waste your time with them?"

"They're not all like that. Delsey's friends sound like good normal families except that they're rich. And she was very careful to say that 95% of the residents are quiet and just want to be left alone. It's the other 5% who cause the trouble."

"Can't you avoid them?"

"Not till I find out who or what killed Kim Taubin. Dr. Andy Bradstreet might have had a motive to kill Manny – not Kim – because he was in love with Manny's wife. On the other hand, Dr. Bradstreet told me, a perfect stranger, that he felt as if Kim had 'stabbed' him when she married Manny. Maybe the poison was intended for Kim."

"What poison? You don't know if Kim was poisoned."

"True – I'm grabbing at anything. Efrem Bronstyn told me Kim declined his invitation to paint her nude. That's not a reason for murder. But his wife Melanie's a different story. She and Kim were bitter enemies over the cherry blossoms."

"For God's sake, Hallie, can you hear yourself?"

"I know, I know. I'm just looking for motives. I suppose even Zelda Rhinehart would have a motive, since she was so worried about this book. But not the two gay women I met. They steer clear of all the quibbling. They told me Kim was the only neighbor who came to their wedding, so they liked her a lot and wanted to pay their respects."

"You know, honey," said Cas in a softer voice, "you're getting in over your head here. It seems there's more anger and hostility beneath the surface than there should be. Who's this guy Willroch Kim wrote about?"

"I haven't had the pleasure. Delsey can't stand him but apparently he has his own coterie of fans."

"Unbelievable how adults can be so childish. Maybe you should think twice about finishing Kim's book."

"Can't, darling, I'm committed – or maybe I should be. Speaking of Delsey, wasn't that rather a long hug you gave her as we were leaving?"

"Ummm – she's not unattractive. But that's the beginning and end of it. I've always been true to you and I always will be. Why would I stray when I've got the best there is?"

"Nice try, sweetheart. But I'm still going to tell her that you snore like a fog horn."

— Chapter 35 —

"I HAVE NEWS – got a minute?" Helen Kaiser's voice brought a smile to Hallie's face on a Monday evening in late April. Two weeks had passed since they'd talked, shortly after Kim's Memorial Service.

Hallie saved the work on her computer and sat up instantly. "I have unlimited minutes for my favorite Police Captain."

"And the only Police Captain you know, right? Have you been working on the Taubin case?"

"I had to take a break. Danny had an ear infection. But yes, I'm trying to finish Kim's book as we speak. What's the news?"

"Huntington Court had a homeowners' meeting yesterday at Manny's house. They meet at 6 p.m. on the last Sunday of every month. Five residents sit on their board, including Manny and your friend Delsey – and they were all there, along with two spouses."

"Go on."

"This morning, Manny went to look for a jewelry box that belonged to Kim. He'd put it aside to give to Kim's sister, Jessica, who was going home to Salem, Oregon this afternoon. The box was gone."

"Hold on, you're going too fast. When had Manny last seen it?"

"Ah, sharp as always. Kim apparently wasn't a jewelry person but Manny had bought her some costly pieces. So before leaving to go running Friday morning, he took a tiny jewelry box with a pair of ruby and diamond earrings, and hid them in a drawer in his dresser. His housekeeper, Ling, apparently saw the box when she put away some handkerchiefs. She insists she didn't open it or peek inside."

"Was the jewelry there after Ling left?"

"Yes, Manny said the earrings were still in the box the next day, Saturday morning. He didn't look for the box again until Monday morning – today."

"And it was gone?"

"Box and all. He was going to give it to Jessica when he picked her up and drove her to the airport. She knew nothing about it, so he didn't say anything. But as soon as he got home, he called our non-emergency number. The officer recognized his name, alerted me, and I phoned Manny."

"And?"

"Manny was quite upset. He remembers placing the box in the drawer on Friday, hiding it under his white handkerchiefs, and checking it Saturday morning. The box was still there. That was the last time he saw it."

"Did he open the box?"

"Yes, the earrings were there."

"Isn't the dresser the first place burglars look?"

"Precisely. A thief once told me they go right for the bedroom – the underwear drawer, under the mattress, or the highest closet shelves."

Hallie exhaled a soft whistle. "Do we know the value? Were the earrings insured?"

"No and no. But my guess is six figures. Two of my men are there now, taking the report. Manny was adamant that the case not be classified as 'Lost Property,' but as 'Theft.' That's when property's been stolen with no sign of illegal entry. As soon as my officers get a description and all the info, we'll track the gems through our nationwide database that checks pawn shop receivables. It's a longshot – but who knows?"

— Chapter 36 —

HALLIE TOOK a moment to absorb the story, then she asked Helen Kaiser, "How can I help you?"

"Is Danny okay?"

"He's fine, thanks."

"Excellent. Aren't you planning to interview some residents for that book you're working on? Is anyone on the

Huntington Court board having financial problems? Could one of them have left during the meeting and gone upstairs? Maybe your friend Delsey has some ideas. By the way, we're keeping this out of the press. Manny doesn't want any more publicity and he doesn't want us bothering his board members. He's not telling anyone what was in the box and neither are we."

"Good idea."

"I want to turn this over to burglary, but TB thinks it could be connected to Kim's death. I promised to wait a few days before doing anything."

"Hmmm. I can't see officer TB chasing a jewel thief. It's not in his self-image."

Helen chuckled. "I know you two have your differences, but he does solve more murders than anyone else. And you've helped with quite a few of them."

"I'm glad someone appreciates me." Hallie laughed. "Thanks for alerting me, Helen, I'd like to talk to some of the neighbors – tactfully, I promise. May I say I'm working with the police?"

"As a volunteer, yes."

"Well, then – I'm on it!"

— Chapter 37 —

A CALL to Delsey half an hour later brought no help. Her answering machine gave the number of her personal assistant, Francie Fisher, who told Hallie that Delsey was off to Hawaii for the week. Since Delsey was the board secretary, however, she had taken minutes at the meeting. Francie would type up Delsey's notes and email them to Hallie within the hour.

The Board of Directors' agenda was as underwhelming as expected. Hallie scanned the minutes quickly. In attendance were all five board members: President Melanie Bronstyn, Secretary Delsey de Baubery, Treasurer Bart Willroch, plus Dr. Rube Rubin and Manny Taubin. Spouses Efrem Bronstyn and Christina Willroch were there as guests.

Hallie was pleased to see that Dr. Rubin was back in town; perhaps she could interview him for Kim's book.

And Bart Willroch? If he was the "asshole, bigot, anti-Semite" Kim had described in her notes, what was he doing on the board?

Although Bart had declined to be interviewed by Kim Taubin, he had no excuse to turn down Hallie, did he? She would proceed in her self-titled role as "acting police investigator."

— Chapter 38 —

THE NEXT DAY, the last Tuesday in April, Hallie decided her first step should be to call on Manny Taubin. Explaining that she was working on the theft, she promised that her late afternoon visit would be short and confidential.

The former quarterback greeted her at his front door, wearing robe and slippers, and sporting a new black moustache and beard. He stood tall and slim, with thick arm muscles bulging under the terry cloth. His face was square-shaped, his forehead wrinkled, his eyes apologetic under bushy brows. The warm smile was still there.

"Sorry for the way I look," were his first words. "I just had a massage. I got this new gal – my financial guy found her on Twiggle or whatever you call it." He reached in his pocket and handed her a card. "She gave me these to give away if you want an awesome massage."

"You look terrific." Hallie tucked the card in her purse and returned his smile. "It's wonderful that you keep in shape. I was so sorry to hear about your robbery."

She followed him into the living room, glad to see it was back to its pristine neatness. "I don't understand people," he said, pointing her to a chair. "How could someone I know be so friggin' mean only a month after I lost my wife? By the way, that funeral business is a real ripoff. I wanna be castrated when I kick off."

"I think you mean cremated."

He laughed. "Oh, yeah."

"Did you say you think the thief was someone you know?"

"Hadda be. I hid the jewelry on Friday mornin', before I went runnin'. Our housekeeper, Ling, was here but no one else. She said she saw the box but didn't touch it. I trust her. The earrings were there on Saturday. Sunday evening, we had the board meetin'. On Monday mornin', I went to get the box I'd hidden and it was gone. Ling couldn't have taken it, so it hadda be someone on our board."

"You discovered the theft yesterday, Monday. And your masseuse didn't come till today, so that lets her off as a suspect. In other words, no one but the board members were in your house from Saturday morning when the jewels were there until Monday noon when you discovered them missing?"

He shook his head. "Correct."

"And you've told nobody what was in the box?"

"Not a livin' soul except for the cops and the police lady, Captain somethin'."

"Kaiser. I'd like to talk to Ling, if okay with you. Manny," she said gently, "mind if I ask a question about Kim?"

"Hell no, I don't mind. I'm offerin' 10 grand to find out why she died."

"Did she have any enemies besides Melanie Bronstyn?"

"Nah, I don't remember crap like that. Ask Delsey. Hey, got a few more minutes? Lemme show ya 'round."

— Chapter 39 —

AFTER A QUICK tour of the large house, with emphasis on the owner's football trophies, Hallie shook hands, thanked her host, and promised to keep him informed.

Driving home, she remembered seeing a guest bathroom at the foot of the staircase. How easy, she thought, for someone to excuse him or herself, presumably to use the restroom, then to sneak upstairs, steal the box, slip it into a purse or pocket, and return to the living room. But how would he or she have known where to find it?

And with Manny's reputation as a womanizer, isn't it possible he entertained a "friend" Saturday night? Maybe whoever took it thought it was so small Manny might think he misplaced it. Or could Manny have forgotten that he moved the box to a different place, and it will turn up later?

Intuition told her otherwise. Manny had been too precise in pointing out the exact drawer, with its small stack of white handkerchiefs. When she asked who ironed them, he'd written down a phone number for Ling, the maid.

Ling-Yee Soong's voice sounded frightened. Her English was limited but she managed to explain that she'd worked for the Taubins for three years and, "Never trouble, no trouble."

Yes, she had noticed a small gray box in the handkerchief drawer that Friday, and no, she hadn't opened it or seen what was in it.

Hallie suspected Ling was lying about not opening it. Who wouldn't be curious about an unlocked jewelry box suddenly turning up in a drawer? Could she have mentioned its existence to the wrong person? Possibly a boyfriend?

Further questioning turned up the fact that Ling worked for other families in Huntington Court, and she would gladly tell Hallie their names if she needed references: Melanie Bronstyn, Christina Willroch, Zelda Rhinehart and Sharon Sampson.

— Chapter 40 —

IT TOOK COURAGE, the next day, for Hallie to contact the detested – at least by Kim – Bart Willroch. Hallie called him at his bank in Laurel Village, a popular shopping area for those who lived in or near the circle. As soon as she told his assistant that she was working with the police on a robbery at Huntington Court, she was put right through to him.

At first, Bart Willroch was anxious and abrupt. After quick assurance that it was not his house that had been robbed, he turned on the "possible-client" charm and invited her to his office.

Chase-Fargo Bank was a modern building with well-dressed "hosts" at the door, welcoming all who entered. A cheerful group of tellers sat or stood behind Lucite screens, assisting customers. Across a central aisle, the VIP bankers held court in private cubicles.

Directed to the waiting section, Hallie stopped by a table offering bottled water and a coffee machine, but had no time to partake. A dark-suited man with reddish-brown hair came hurrying toward her. He was freckled and pleasant looking, save for the beard stubble which the younger generation seemed to think attractive.

"Ms. Marsh?" They shook hands. "Bart Willroch at your service. Please come in, have a seat."

Sizing him up from the back as he walked, she noticed that he was of medium height, about 5-foot-9. His custom-tailored suit fit to perfection, and reminded her of Cas's warning, "Don't worry about a guy's clothes, look at his shoes. If you see tassels, head for the nearest exit." The banker's highly polished wingtips passed the test.

Inside his small, well-furnished office, he moved a chair towards her, flashing a smile. "Nice to meet you, Ms. Marsh."

"Please call me Hallie. I won't stay long." She watched

as he seated himself behind a desk neatly arranged with papers and electronic machines.

"To save time," he began, "I'll explain that after you phoned, I took the liberty of calling my neighbor Melanie Bronstyn to ask about the robbery. She called Manny Taubin to get the story, but all he told her was that something valuable was missing – no details. That's all I know and that was the first I'd heard of it until you called me today. Melanie said you're helping the police solve Kim Taubin's death. Do you think she was murdered?"

— Chapter 41 —

The question caught Hallie off guard. "I – honestly don't know, Mr. Willroch."

"Bart. And you didn't come here to talk about jewelry. You want to talk about murder, right?"

"Well, I admit I wanted to meet you. Kim's description of you in her book notes was less than flattering. Do you know anything about her death?"

He smiled. "No, I know about her book and I definitely do not want to be in it, but I couldn't stop her from photographing our house. I did not kill her. I do not hate Jewish people, or any other race or ethnic minority. Some of my best friends worship at the nearby temple, and they were the ones who started calling our little corner of heaven 'Circumcision Circle.' Kim thought I started that and refused to listen to reason. What else do you want to know?"

"Is that why she disliked you?"

"The feeling was mutual. Kim was a major pain in the butt, always complaining about her damn allergies, as if she's the only one with health problems. Just because she had the sneezies every spring, we should uproot our world-famous trees? No way! I told her to go on a cruise or take a trip somewhere if she wanted to escape the pollens. Why destroy our beautiful cherry blossoms and penalize 22 families because of her own selfish wishes?"

Hallie nodded and moved on. "I take it you and Melanie Bronstyn are good friends."

His answer was almost too casual. "Naturally we're good friends. We're on the board together, with Manny, Dr. Rubin, and Delsey. Melanie was absolutely right to fight Kim. Those trees mean a lot to us. Kim's gone now. I had nothing to do with her demise, but I can't say I'm shedding tears. Anything else?"

"Just one thing more. A woman named Ling cleans your house?"

"Ling? What a character! Loves to gossip. My wife, Christina, gets all the latest news from her."

"About what?"

"Everything. Say, if you need a cleaning woman, Ling's excellent and quite reasonable." He reached for a card on his desk, and scribbled a number. "Give Christina a call. She'll give Ling a fine reference."

PART 6

Relieved to have the meeting over, Hallie climbed into her car and headed home. By now, she'd met Efrem Bronstyn, the artist with the face scar, chatted with the gay women, and called on Bart Willroch. He was not the ogre she expected, and in fact, she believed his story and found his directness refreshing.

Except for Dr. Harvey Rubin, who apparently flew to Hawaii the day after the board meeting, she could now write a short, impersonal paragraph about each Huntington Court family, and finish the damn book.

Back at her desk that afternoon, Hallie scolded herself for having asked Bart about Kim's death when she'd promised Helen Kaiser she would focus on the jewelry theft. Reliving his remarks about the maid, she wondered…if Ling was such a gossip, what was she was gossiping about?

Christina Willroch's recorded voice announced that she was "not available" and that, "I will return the call at my earliest convenience." A strange distortion of the phrase, but probably accurate.

Checking her emails, Hallie found a new message from Police Captain Kaiser: "As you requested, we ran background checks on all the Huntington Court residents. No outstanding arrest warrants, no big scandals. Vance Ferlingetty had four DUI's some years ago, but I'm told he's bedridden now.

"Also, we found an article on Dr. Harvey Rubin. Twelve years ago, he worked at a hospital in Maine. Seems that one of his patients, age 19, had ALS, Lou Gehrig's Disease. In constant pain, the boy and his parents begged Rubin to end his suffering – and his life. The doctor obliged, but his sympathy cost him his license. He came west, got a California license to practice medicine, and made a new start.

"Then, of course, there's Manny Taubin, who paid off the stripper who socked him with a paternity suit 10 years ago. You probably read about it. The boy was eight at the time. For all we know, Manny might still be paying child support."

"Omigod!" Hallie gasped, typed out a few words, and hit the send key. Her query was short and direct: "Manny Taubin has a son?"

— Chapter 43 —

HELEN KAISER responded to Hallie's question with a phone call. "We can't find any info on Manny Junior right now. He probably has another name. Or maybe he and his mother left the country. We're still making inquiries. Any news on the robbery?"

"No," Hallie said. "Has Kim's tox screen come back yet? Any word from the pawn shops?"

The Captain's terse negative answer told Hallie her friend was tired and overworked, as always, and had no time for chatting.

The next morning, Thursday, Christina Willroch returned Hallie's call. Their maid/housekeeper Ling was coming to work at their home, 6 Huntington Court, on Saturday, and

Christina would be happy to have Hallie stop by and talk to the woman any time between "nine and two." Hallie left word that she appreciated the courtesy and would be there at ten.

— Chapter 44 —

SIX HUNTINGTON COURT was a handsome beige-stucco home with an arched roof over a short walkway to the front door. According to Delsey, Bart Willroch had a client who went bankrupt about 20 years ago, and through some secret – and probably illegal – manipulations, Bart was able to buy the house for $3 million. Today, Delsey guessed, it was worth four times that amount.

Bart liked to claim the house was built by San Francisco's most famous architect, the late Willis Polk. His signature slate roof, Bart insisted, was proof positive.

Not so, according to Kim. Her soon-to-be-finished book made very clear that City Hall records showed the design was the work of a copycat architect named James Haeberly, also deceased. Polk's name was not mentioned.

Still, Hallie noted as she drove up, the house was built to impress, and impress it did. Lovingly kept lawns, spring flowers and tall magnolia trees guarded the façade, adding to its lush exterior.

A shapely blonde in white tennis shorts answered the bell almost immediately. "Hi, Hallie," she said, offering her hand, "I'm Christina, and I apologize for the dark glasses. Just had some work done – you know how that is."

"You look fine to me. Off to exercise?"

"I am, yes. I play with my good friend Dagmar Millard every Saturday, and sometimes Lisa Newman joins us. She's president of the Symphony this year. I hope you're coming to our opening in September. It's going to be over the top."

"I'll be there. My mother, Edith Marsh, always buys a box for the family." What the hell, Hallie thought. I can play the name-drop game, too.

"Oh? I wondered if you were related. She's such a wonderful woman, so generous to the arts. Please, come inside. I've three minutes before my driver arrives."

— Chapter 45 —

THE INTERIOR of 6 Huntington Court was no less than expected. The first thing that caught Hallie's eyes was a dramatic spiral staircase with marble steps. At its base, a veneered cabinet with glass doors showed off a collection of snuff bottles, jade figurines and Limoges boxes. Christina walked quickly past it, taking Hallie's arm and chatting non-stop.

At first glance, the living room seemed overburdened with art objects and antiques. It was Mumsy's taste, Hallie thought. How she would love that Corot landscape on the wall, or the pair of vintage side tables with their dainty Chinoiserie finish.

Mumsy would not love the bronze anatomically-correct male torso, but neither did Hallie. That had to be the work of Efrem Bronstyn.

76

"What a lovely room!" She perched on the edge of a chair.

"Isn't it?" Christina seated herself on a couch and reached for a small decorated container. "I love this papier mâché tea caddy from the 1800s. It's one of a kind, worth a fortune. Belonged to my great grandmother."

"Amazing," said Hallie. Determined to make the most of her three minutes, she added, "but I know you have to leave and I'd love to hear more about Ling. Your husband says she's a bit of a gossip."

"For sure, she's a wealth of information about the other residents. I often wonder how much she tells them about me. But I like to think she's loyal and I do trust her. Bart's at the bank today, so she'll be alone in the house. Naturally, I lock up my diamonds."

"Did you know Kim Taubin?"

"A nice girl. Not a friend, but I felt sorry for her. Everyone knew that Manny – well, you know – liked the ladies. So sad. I don't know why Bart disliked Kim so much. When we –"

"Your car is here, Miss Clisty," called a voice.

"Already? Oh, dear." She jumped to her feet. "You must come back sometime, Hallie, and bring your wonderful mother. I'd love to meet her."

"Thanks, that's kind of you." Hallie rose as her host ran to the door. "Good luck on the courts!"

— **Chapter 46** —

WATCHING through a window, Hallie saw Christina Willroch hurry towards a shiny white Jaguar. A uniformed chauffeur tipped his hat and helped her into the back seat. Uber it wasn't.

"You want talk to me?" A voice broke into her thoughts. She turned to see a young woman with jet black hair and Chinese features. Her hands were shaking visibly.

"I am Ling-Yee Soong, call me Ling," she said bowing. "You Miss Hah-ri?"

"Yes, whatever. Now please relax. I am your friend. Understand?"

"I have to clean house. What you want?"

Hallie sighed silently. "Ling, you clean many houses, talk to many people. Do you know the word gossip?"

A smile crossed the maid's face. "I like gossip. I talk too much."

"People like you to gossip, Ling. Can you tell me what you talk about?"

"No." She shook her head, then eyed her questioner warily. "Why you want gossip?"

Patiently, Hallie explained about the missing box. "I know you saw it last Friday when you cleaned the Taubins' house. Did you tell anyone about it?"

Ling frowned. "I know nothing! I clean Miss Clisty and Miss Sampson house next day, Saturday. I tell them about strange box in drawer and they ask if I look inside. I say no, I no see nothing." She paused to state emphatically, "I not steal joo-ry!"

— Chapter 47 —

LING'S DENIAL of having peeked in the box was somewhat dimmed by her reference to jewelry, since the contents of the box had not been mentioned.

Sensing the young woman was being less than truthful, Hallie questioned her for another hour, finally gaining her trust and learning that a) the Rhineharts fought about his drinking, and he was nicer than she; b) the gay couple wanted to adopt an African-American baby, but feared what the neighbors would say; c) Mr. Willroch often yelled at his wife for spending too much money; and d) Melanie Bronstyn tried to discourage Efrem from painting nudes, while Efrem accused his wife of "flirting" with Bart Willroch.

Poor Ling must be lonely, Hallie concluded, to pass along so much personal information. She insisted she had no boyfriend, though she admitted she'd like one. Obviously, spreading gossip gave her a sense of importance.

— Chapter 48 —

"I SPOKE to Ling, the Taubins' maid," Hallie reported to Captain Kaiser. She admitted seeing the box in Manny's handkerchief drawer, but insisted she didn't open it."

"Did you feel she was 1 lying?"

"I'm pretty sure she was. I'll follow up."

A quick call to Manny Taubin confirmed that he hadn't told anyone about the box's contents. Driving to visit her mother,

Hallie reviewed what she knew about the robbery.

Who were the suspects? Ling left the Taubins' house Friday. The jewelry was there Saturday morning, so Ling didn't take it. Manny found the box missing Monday morning, before his masseuse arrived. So the masseuse couldn't have taken it.

Assuming neither Manny nor Delsey were the culprits, the thief had to be one of the other three board members who were there that Sunday night: Dr. Rubin, Melanie Bronstyn, Bart Willroch, or one of their two spouses – Efrem Bronstyn and Christina Willroch.

Was the theft connected to Kim's death? It didn't seem likely.

Melanie and Bart were probably hooking up, Hallie concluded, and Kim hated them both. If Kim knew about the affair, might they (Melanie and Bart) fear that she'd hint about it in her book? Might Bart want to keep her from writing that Willis Polk was not the architect who designed their house? That would make a huge difference in the home's value.

What about Zelda Rhinehart who worried that Kim's book might mention her incarcerated sons? And then there was Dr. Andy Bradstreet who felt "stabbed" when Kim told him she was getting married.

Could any of these be motives for murder?

— Chapter 49 —

HALLIE'S THOUGHTS were interrupted by the chime of her

cell phone. Pulling to the curb, she saw the call came from the SFPD, the San Francisco Police Department.

"It's me, Helen," said the Captain. "I have bad news. TB and Lenny were chasing a murder suspect, when the guy turned around and shot them. Hit TB in the shoulder. He's in surgery now."

"How awful!" Hallie exclaimed. "I'm so sorry! Will he be okay?"

"We think so. I'm on my way to the hospital. I wish I hadn't been bitchy to him this morning. I told him if he didn't like the way I run my office, he should transfer."

"Don't feel guilty. I'm sure that had nothing to do with his being shot."

"I know – thanks. TB has no family, so I'm staying with him now till he's out of danger. By the way, I have 2 tickets to a gun control dinner tonight. The Chief's wife asked me to buy the darn things and I couldn't say no. Would you consider going and representing me?"

"Were you supposed to speak?"

"No. Senator Anna Steinberg's giving the keynote. Doesn't she live in Huntington Court?"

"Yes, she does. I'll call Cas at the office and call you right back."

— Chapter 50 —

"COUNT ME OUT!" Cas's voice was strong and clear. "We're on deadline, honey, and I'll be working till 8 or 9 o'clock. We've got a PICNIC problem."

"A What?"

"One of my reporters keeps telling me his machine is broken, and yet it works fine for me. We call that a PICNIC: Problem In Chair, Not In Computer."

Hallie laughed. "That sounds familiar."

"You know how I hate to go to those dinners, anyway, especially where they start asking you to donate 100 grand, then they go down to 100 bucks, and if you don't give anything, everyone treats you like an outcast."

"Peer pressure. That's why it works. It's called 'Fund a Need.' The money goes for good purposes."

"Then take your checkbook, sweetheart. Take a friend and enjoy. Gotta run." Click.

"Sorry, I have to regret tonight," Hallie told Captain Kaiser, a moment later. "Cas has to work. He's on deadline."

"Would you go with Officer Brisco?"

"Lenny? You mean TB's partner?"

"Yes. He said he'd be happy to escort you. His wife's out of town."

"I don't think that's a good –"

"It's important to me, Hallie. My best homicide inspector just got shot by a crazed gunman. You know how I feel about my officers' safety. I want to be represented at that dinner."

"Oh, shoot! – uh, no pun intended." She sighed. "Okay, boss-lady, when and where?"

— Chapter 51 —

OFFICER LENNY BRISCO showered, shaved, dressed in his best suit and tie, and rang the doorbell of the woman of his dreams at 7 p.m. that Saturday night. He knew he was in love with Hallie Marsh; he had been for at least five years, since the day they met.

In his mind, she was "the angel" – as beautiful inside as she was in person. He also knew there was no hope of a romance, or even a one-night stand. Women like that were loyal, loving, and monogamous. They didn't fool around.

Did she know how he felt? Did she even suspect? He doubted it. The fluttering in his stomach told him he was nervous. His brain told him not to say or do anything that might offend…to restrain whatever impulses he might have as the evening progressed. He mustn't allow himself a drink, not a single one. If he lost control even for three seconds, he could say goodbye to his career.

"Hi, Lenny. Wow, you clean up well!" Hallie kissed the detective's cheek, linked arms and walked with him to his car. "So nice of you to put up with me tonight."

He gulped silently, speechless. She was wearing a form-fitting wool dress which showed off her slim figure. "You – look good, too," he finally mumbled. "I'm a bit nervous, sort of like taking out the boss's wife."

"Well, please forget that I know the Captain, and relax. I'm not going to report on you, just on the dinner – unless you get drunk and dance on the tables or something. How's TB?"

Relieved to change subjects, he helped her into the car and resisted the impulse to strap her in. "Uhhh – where are we going?" he asked, slipping into the driver's seat. "I seem to have forgotten."

— Chapter 52 —

HALLIE LAUGHED SOFTLY. "We're going to the good old St.Francis Hotel. Bush Street's the best. What about TB?"

"The doctor said the surgery went well. They removed the bullet but the impact caused a blockage in the carotid artery on the side of his neck. They had to insert a stent – a tiny tube – to open the artery and get the blood flowing to his brain so he won't have a stroke. I think I got that right. The doctor says he'll have a complete recovery."

"That's wonderful news. What about the crazy guy?"

"I had to shoot him in the leg or he'd have killed us both. He'll live to shoot again, unfortunately. I'm in favor of making all guns illegal – except for cops, that is. Isn't that what tonight's about?"

"Sort of, Lenny. Senator Steinberg's going to speak. I heard her talk on this subject before. She told how she was getting threats when she first entered politics, so she got a gun permit and learned how to shoot. As time went on and gun violence increased, she changed her mind and asked the public to turn in their handguns. She turned in her own, and they were all melted down and sculpted into a cross. Then she flew to Rome and presented it to the Pope."

"Good story, if true." Lenny felt himself starting to

unwind. "What if the Pope could talk to God and make all the guns in the world disappear. Wouldn't that be terrific?"

"God would have to change human nature, too."

"Oh," said Lenny, nodding. "Well, then, it probably won't happen."

PART 7

THE WESTIN St. Francis' Colonial Ballroom was packed with business and legal professionals, as well as advocates for smart gun laws from around the country. The cocktail hour dragged for Hallie, who sipped her Bloody Mary, and was a captive listener to Lenny's life story.

Across the room she spotted her lawyer, Nate Garchik, chatting with a blonde who had her back to the crowd. Nate waved, and Hallie blew a kiss.

She and Lenny stood by themselves in the large ballroom, apart from the mob of unfamiliar faces. "Say," he said, after a brief silence, "Did I tell you about the time I screwed up my lines in Hamlet?"

No sooner had he spoken, than Hallie noticed that Nate's blonde friend was heading for the restrooms. She looked familiar. "Lenny, will you excuse me a minute? I'm going to say hello to a friend, and I'll meet you right back here."

Hurrying across the floor, Hallie caught up with the woman at the door to the ladies' room. She was designer-dressed and carrying a showy purse, obviously Chanel. "Christina Willroch? Is that you?"

The blonde spun around. "Hallie? What are you doing here? Bart drags me to this boring dinner every year. If I had my way, I'd sleep with a loaded gun under my pillow. How's a girl supposed to protect herself?"

Not waiting for an answer, she continued, "Bart tied a bow in the back of my jacket and it came undone. Would you mind re-tying it for me?"

"Happy to." Hallie looked closer. "It's going to come un-done again unless we attach it. I've a safety pin in my purse."

Christina shrank back. "No – no thanks! I'm allergic to pins and needles. I had a bad time when I was little, with a nurse trying to get into my veins. She held me down while I screamed in pain – then I passed out. I haven't been able to look at a needle ever since."

"Goodness! How do you get shots? Blood tests?"

"It's awful. They have to knock me out with laughing gas or valium before they can come near me. It's a real ailment called trypanophobia. One person in 10 has it."

"Has anyone tried to desensitize you?"

"It didn't work. So if you don't mind, Hallie, just tie a pretty bow and I'll go back to my table."

— Chapter 54 —

CAS WAS STANDING at the window when Lenny Brisco drove Hallie home and walked her to the door. With a thank-you and a quick peck on her escort's cheek, she turned the key and hurried inside.

"Who the hell was that?" Cas asked, greeting his wife with a frown.

"Didn't you get my note?"

"Yes, but who the hell is Lenny?"

"He's TB's partner. TB's the homicide inspector who's always giving me a bad time. You said he needs to get laid. Remember?"

"I wasn't offering my wife."

"I'm talking about TB, not Lenny. Lenny's happily married but his wife's out of town."

"How convenient."

Hallie rolled her eyes. "You can't possibly be jealous of Lenny. All he did was talk about himself the whole evening."

"He was trying to impress you. I saw the way he looked at you."

"Cas, for God's sake!"

He sighed. "Okay, okay, I guess I'm tired. How was the dinner?"

"Perfect. A 13-year old girl talked about how her best friend was shot and killed. Everyone was crying. Well, I was, anyway. And then the Senator – Anna Steinberg – told why she wrote the assault weapons ban more than a decade ago, and how the NRA has a stranglehold on Congress. She's very passionate on the subject."

"Did you meet her?"

"I went up to her afterwards – she was surrounded by admirers. I squeezed in and told her I was working on a book about Huntington Court. She said that was nice, but she was putting her house on the market. I didn't have a chance to ask any questions, damn it."

Cas put his arm around his wife and smiled. "Sorry I got jealous, honey. It's just that I love you so much."

"And you can't wait to call one of your reporters to find out why the Senator is selling her house, right?"

"Bless you, my child." He turned and ran up the stairs.

Chapter 55

THE INVITATION to breakfast a few mornings later delighted Hallie. Delsey de Baubery, just back from Hawaii, was anxious to hear what she'd missed.

Hallie stirred her Constant Comment as they sat at Delsey's lace-covered table. "Your tan looks terrific," she said, "but my mother's always getting skin cancers from all the sunbathing she used to do."

"I know – and I do wear sunscreen." Delsey opened her palms. "It just doesn't last."

"You had a good trip?"

"Incredible!"

"Relaxing?"

"More or less."

"Hmm, I see. Were you alone?"

"Not exactly."

"Anyone I know?"

"No, you've never met him."

"Why do I feel like I'm pulling teeth?"

"I'm being stupid." Delsey reddened. "I wasn't going to tell anybody, but…I met Harvey there."

Hallie's eyes widened. "Harvey? The invisible rabbit?"

"Harvey Rubin, my neighbor. We've been seeing each other. We planned a secret rendezvous, away from prying eyes. But now that I think about it, we're both adults and we're both single. Why do we bother to hide our relationship?"

"Probably because you live in a beehive of gossipers."

"And because it's nobody's business." She brightened. "I

told Harvey all about you, how you were finishing Kim's book, and how you were helping find out what happened to her. He's anxious to meet you."

"And vice versa. All I know about him is that he's a widower, and a compassionate doctor who helped a boy out of his misery and lost his license somewhere –"

"Maine. He's the sweetest, kindest man who ever lived. He cares about people – not just his patients. You'll meet him soon. Now I need you to tell me what's happening here. Any news about Kim?"

"No, the case is still open. Cause of death is on hold till we get the tox screen. But we did have a bit of a problem..."

— Chapter 56 —

HALLIE STAYED long enough to get Delsey up to date on the jewelry theft, then asked if she would call Dr. Rubin for her. Five minutes with him, and she could finish the book.

Delsey dialed his private number. He was about to leave for his office, but since Hallie was visiting at 16 Huntington Court and the doctor lived at number 12, she could walk over for a brief chat. At last!

The façade of number 12 featured light gray shingles and three black-trimmed windows sharing an iron balcony. If Hallie remembered right, Kim's notes said that the rectangular three-story building blended the Prairie School influence with Mediterranean motifs. Or was it Elizabethan? Was Charles Whittlesey or Julia Morgan the architect? Each home was different. How could anyone remember who designed what?

Ringing the doorbell, she had only to wait seconds before it was answered.

"Come in, come in." A tall, husky man with a black patch over one eye offered a firm handshake. His voice was warm and direct. "Delsey's told me so much about you. She didn't exaggerate about your beauty. But I didn't know I'd be enjoying it so soon."

"Thanks, Dr. Rubin. I just learned about you two a few minutes ago. I think it's wonderful."

Hallie beamed approvingly and tried not to seem as if she were looking him over, which she was. An appealing, clean-shaven man, he had classic features and straight gray hair combed back from his forehead. A well-worn suit with a skinny tie told her he was the antithesis of Delsey's fashion plate ex-husband, Ashton Crocklebank.

"My friends call me Rube," said the doctor, leading her down the hall past stacks of lumber, paint cans and several workmen. "Delsey says it sounds like a gangster's name. I like to think of Rube Goldberg who invented all those brilliant machines. Excuse my bachelor pad."

He opened a door to a den filled with floor-to-ceiling bookcases. Magazines, newspapers and papers lay in piles on the carpet. A wooden desk was buried under computer equipment, files, clippings, and framed pictures.

Gesturing towards one of two folding chairs, he explained, "I can't invite you into my living room because Delsey's contractor is fixing it up for me. She insists my house needs a woman's touch. I told her she could do whatever she

92

wants in any room except this one. It's disorganized, cluttered and messy – but it's my sanctuary."

— **Chapter 57** —

HALLIE SETTLED into her seat while her host kept talking: "The first thing most people want to ask me is why I wear an eye patch. Do you care?"

"I'm curious. I'd never ask you, though."

The doctor sank into an armchair behind his desk. "Sometimes I have fun with it. I've a full repertoire of stories – my favorite is that I lost 50% of my sight on an African safari, saving a young woman from the jaws of an alligator. The truth is that an inept surgeon bungled an operation for a torn retina."

"That's terrible! Did you sue him?"

"What for? It wouldn't bring back my sight." He ran his fingers through his hair. "Now look, I understand you're finishing Kim Taubin's book. What information do you need from me?"

"Did you know Kim?"

"Yes."

"Did you like her?"

"No. Don't tell Delsey I said this, but she was a spoiled, self-centered young woman." He paused a moment. "I wasn't going to tell you any more, but in light of what's happened, I think you deserve to know."

He waited another moment, brushed back his hair again, then spoke softly. "Two years ago, Kim Taubin was driving around the circle on her way home. She was going fast and didn't see Bella, my wife, crossing the street. Bella was carrying our Yorkie, Spunky, in her purse, as she always did."

Hallie nodded, fearing what she was about to hear.

"Bella stopped suddenly to keep from getting run over, and Spunky fell out of her purse to the pavement. Kim hit her brakes just in time, saw that Bella was unhurt, waved an apology and drove on – right over Spunky."

"Oh, no! Did Kim stop?"

"Yes, she did. She knew she'd hit something. She jumped out of the car, saw the dead dog and apologized to Bella, but Bella was in shock and couldn't even speak. We couldn't have children, you see, and for five years, that cuddly little doggie had gotten all her maternal love and attention."

"What did Kim do?"

"She wasn't a dog person and she didn't understand that for Bella, it was almost like losing a child. Kim tried to make light of the accident, and made the mistake of offering to drive Bella to the pet store and buy her another dog."

"Oh, dear."

"My darling Bella was inconsolable – and hysterical. She ran home and called me at my office. I arranged for my partner to see my patients and drove right here. Spunky – what was left of him – was strewn all over the street. I gathered most of the body parts. It was worse than you can imagine."

— **Chapter 58** —

WITH A LOUD SIGH, Rube continued, "The next day we

94

had a funeral for Spunky in our garden."

"Was Delsey there?" asked Hallie.

"No, I didn't know her then. We bought another pure-bred Yorkie, but he just reminded Bella of Spunky, and we had to return him. Bella went into a severe depression. She never recovered from that experience and died a few months later. The official cause of death was heart failure. A broken heart. I haven't wanted to have anything to do with Kim Taubin since then."

"Understandable!" Hallie tried to sort out her thoughts. Had she stumbled on another motive for Kim's death? Rube was a medical doctor trained to "never do harm" and save lives.

Yet according to Helen Kaiser, he had helped a suffering, terminally-ill teenager end his life. Was that an act of mercy or a breach of the Hippocratic Oath? Could taking the life of a woman he considered selfish, insensitive, and a menace to others, be justified in his mind?

"Last year," Rube continued, "Melanie Bronstyn asked me to join the board with Manny Taubin. I tried to get out of it, but it was my turn to serve, and I couldn't blame Manny for his wife's actions. I agreed to do my part and I got to know Delsey at the board meetings, so in that sense, it was the right decision."

"I'm happy for you both." She wondered…was Delsey fixing up his house so she could move in? How serious were they?

"Then all I need from you, Rube, is a word or two about your home and Huntington Court."

"Of course, that's why you came here. Can you just say

that I thank the Lord every day that I bought this house when I did? I couldn't possibly afford to buy it today. My neighbors are good people, I've paid off my mortgage, we can park our cars on the street, and when our cherry blossom trees are in bloom, it's one of the most beautiful sights in the city."

"On second thought," he added, "Better not mention the cherry blossoms."

— Chapter 59 —

Hallie was thrilled to add the final chapter to Kim's book. With a mental shout of relief, she emailed the text to the publisher, who already had the pictures and layout.

A call to Delsey confirmed that she and Rube were not serious at that point, and that she had no interest or desire to move in with him. Should they take their relationship to the next level, they would still keep their homes. From Delsey's point of view, living separately was the ideal arrangement.

With the book pressure off, and Kim's tox screen results not due for another week, Hallie decided to focus on the jewelry theft.

Having met Rube, she had felt his deep sadness when he spoke of his late wife. At the same time, she sensed a man of compassion – a need to do what was right, to follow his humanitarian instincts even if they clashed with the law. If she was correct, murder and larceny were not on his agenda.

That left only the Bronstyns and the Willrochs as Sunday night suspects in the jewelry theft, although it still didn't seem logical that horndog Manny would spend the previous night, a Saturday, alone watching TV.

She had an idea.

Delsey had mentioned that their guard comes on duty at five p.m. every day. At ten to five that afternoon, Hallie parked her car inside the Huntington Court gate to wait for him.

He arrived promptly, and the official-looking deputy police card convinced him that Hallie was legitimate, and entitled to see his log of callers on the night of Saturday, April 6th. Although Manny had denied it, there was indeed a visitor to number 21 Huntington Court at 7:20 p.m. And the guard had a license number.

— Chapter 60 —

After stopping at See's candy store for a two-pound box of chocolates, Hallie drove directly to Saint Teresa Hospital, a large modern medical center South of Market Street. She parked and rode the elevator to the second floor.

"May I give this to Sergeant Theodore Baer in 246?" she asked at the nurse's station. "I won't stay long."

A young woman in white shook her head. "The Sergeant isn't seeing visitors," she said. "Try next week."

"Could I just peek in and hand this to him?"

"No —"

"Yes, you can," interrupted a gray-haired nurse who seemed to be in charge. "Mr. Baer is feeling better today and I think a pretty woman bringing candy would cheer him even more."

Thanks – thanks so much." Hallie hurried down the hall before the nurse could change her mind.

— Chapter 61 —

"DO NOT DISTURB" said the sign on the door of room 246. Hallie knocked gently. Getting no response, she twisted the handle and peered inside.

A plastic curtain separated two sections of the room. TB was closest to the door, sitting up in bed staring at the food tray on his lap. His neck, chest, and one arm were wrapped in bandages. "Who's that?" he demanded. "Is that you, Hallie Marsh?"

She sank back, fearing his anger. "I'm sorry, TB, I just wanted to give you this."

"Come in, come in." The detective arched his brows in surprise. "You came to see me?"

"Well, yes. I heard of your bad luck. Are you in pain?"

"Only when I breathe." He motioned to a chair. "I'll be damned. I thought you hated me."

Hallie sat down. Was this conversation really happening? "We've had a few disagreements, but I've always admired you, TB. I'm told you're going to be 100 percent when you heal."

"Is that candy for me?"

"Every last piece. Shall I open it?"

"I'd appreciate. You wouldn't believe the food here. I can't chew worth a damn so they pulverize everything and it all tastes like sh – garbage."

She placed the open box by his unbandaged arm and handed him a chocolate. "This one's a truffle – no nuts. Let it melt in your mouth."

"Mmm, good. What's happening with Kim Taubin? Captain Kaiser won't tell me anything. Says I should concentrate on getting well. Doesn't mean my brain turns off. And Lenny – good old Lenny. He's got a temporary partner he says is even more stubborn than me. But clue me in. What's going on?"

"I just came from Huntington Court —"

"Where?"

"You know, the pretty cul-de-sac where Cas found Kim's body."

"You mean that snobby dead end street?"

"Whatever. Anyway, I learned that Manny Taubin had lied. He had indeed hosted a visitor that Saturday night before the theft, and the guard at the gate gave me a license number. Would you know how I can get an address?"

"Take this." He handed her his phone with his good arm. "Click on the purple app, dial in 466tb where it says 'Code,' then add the license number and check the screen. It should give you all you need."

"God bless technology," she murmured, typing in the code and scrambling in her purse for the card with the license number. Ten seconds after she entered the facts, a name, address, and "Case Summary" page popped up. She promptly emailed the information to herself and handed back the phone. "Thanks, TB, that's a real help."

"Remember, if you screw up, it's my friggin' butt on the grill, young lady. Swear to me that you won't do your usual dumb-ass tricks and go snooping around that address by yourself?"

"Now you sound like the TB I know," she laughed. "I promise."

— Chapter 62 —

HALLIE WAS HOME IN TIME to defrost a Stauffer's Baked Chicken for Cas and toss a salad for herself. She joined him, seated at the kitchen counter.

"I'm pooped," she said, setting down his food. "And I'm hopeful, too. We may have a new robbery suspect – an outsider."

Cas reached for his fork. "Thanks for thawing my dinner, Honey. Who might that be?"

"Let's see. I started the day with breakfast at Delsey's house. She's dating Dr. Rubin – they call him Rube – so I walked over to his house to see him and get a quote. I came home, finished the book, sent it off, then drove Danny to his pre-school."

"I still say Danny's too young."

"He loves it. He needs to be around kids. At five o'clock, I went to Huntington Court and talked to the guard. He showed me his log of guests, and it seems that Manny Taubin did have a visitor that Saturday night – the night before their

Sunday board meeting.

"A lady of the evening, no doubt."

"No doubt. The guard gave me her license number. Then I brought some candy to TB in the hospital."

"Was he thrilled to see you?"

"He was actually pleasant. He even found me a name and address to go with the phone number. Now don't scream, I promised I wouldn't go there alone."

Cas exhaled loudly. "Why couldn't I marry a nice, quiet woman who likes to stay home and make cookies?"

"Ever heard of Barbara Gaine?"

"That's the name that goes with the license?"

"Yes, and as soon as you finish your dinner, we're going to pay her a call."

— **Chapter 63** —

PART OF CAS, the protective husband part, would have instantly declined the invitation to visit Ms. Barbara Gaine. The practical part of him, however, knew that if he did so, Hallie would find someone else to take her to her destination, possibly that fawning cop, Lenny something.

Then, too, the newsman in Cas sniffed a story. What if Ms. Gaine had stolen the jewels? Too bad they couldn't surprise her with a search warrant, but no sane judge would grant one. They hadn't a clue that led to the woman, and not a scrap of evidence linking her to the theft.

"Suppose we go buzz her doorbell," Cas said. "What makes you think she'll let us in and talk to us?"

"I have my Deputy Police card your old girlfriend gave me. And I can say I'm helping the police."

"Helen told you to say that? I'm sure she didn't mean for you to ring strangers' doorbells. Where does Ms. Gaine live?"

"In the Sunset."

"Did you try Googling her?"

"Yes. No luck. But I read that until the 1930s, the Sunset District was sand dunes all the way to Ocean Beach. Did you know that? Today, mostly Asian-Americans live there and there's no crime."

"No crime?"

"Not much, from the statistics. Look, sweetheart, if you don't want to go with me, I could ask my brother Rob. Or better yet, a cop. Maybe I could get Lenny Brisco –"

"What time do you want to leave?"

— **Chapter 64** —

"LET ME DO the talking, please." Hallie reached for her Deputy Police I.D. as Cas pulled into the driveway of a small white stucco house, similar to the other white stucco houses on the block. A noticeable difference was that Barbara Gaine had a wooden fence surrounding her grass by the entrance. Torn dolls and rusty toy cars lay scattered on the neglected lawn.

After several rings, Cas took his wife's arm. "Nobody's here. Let's go home."

"Must be God's will," said Hallie. "We should've stopped to question Manny first. It's only fair to warn him. Let's stop by to see him."

"Now? My watch says 8 o'clock. You can't be serious!"

"Will you drive to 21 Huntington Court or shall I?"

A quick phone call ascertained that Manny Taubin was indeed at home, preparing to go out, but amenable to a five-minute visit.

He stood awaiting his guests in the open doorway. "Hi, guys," he said, "You caught me just in time. What's so friggin' important?"

Cas shook his hand, Hallie pecked his cheek. "You look very handsome in your suit and tie, Manny. We don't need to sit down. I'll get right to the point."

"Sure, angel face. What can I do you for?"

Hallie smiled. "It's not terribly important, Manny, but we learned that you had a woman visitor on that Saturday night, the weekend the jewelry disappeared."

The widower showed no emotion. "Yeah, nice gal. I didn't wanna get her involved." A brief pause and he continued, "It's like this, see. I meet this guy at my gym, and he gives me a sob story about this poor woman who's got two kids and can't pay her mortgage. He says she could give me a body massage for 200 bucks. He says I'd be helpin' someone in need. So she comes over Saturday night and gives me a massage. I pay her the dough, give her a nice tip, and she goes home. No way she could've ripped off my jewelry."

"Why is that?" asked Cas innocently.

Manny grinned. "I know what you guys are thinkin' and you're right. I had my 'massage' on the livin' room floor and she never went upstairs. Never even left the room. She

103

grabbed her coat, went out the door, and I haven't seen or heard from her since."

— Chapter 65 —

Manny Taubin's "confession" ended Cas and Hallie's visit quickly. Hallie's phone call to Ms. Gaine the next morning confirmed that she certainly did recall her date with the famous football hero.

"I did nothing illegal," she told Hallie, who represented herself as a volunteer police deputy. "I work for an escort service, and when my boss told me Manny Taubin needed a date, I canceled my other appointments and jumped at the chance. Who wouldn't want to go out with Manny Taubin!"

"But you didn't go out. You stayed home, right?"

"Yes, I gave him a back rub and we watched a little TV, then he said he was tired, so I left. He was a perfect gentleman. Have you talked to him? Did he like me?"

"I'm afraid he didn't say," said Hallie. "Would you mind telling me where the TV was?"

"In the living room. It looked like an awfully big house. He said he'd give me a tour next time I come over. Didn't he say anything about me?"

"We talked mostly about his wife. Her death is still unexplained, as you may have read."

"I'm a longtime football fan, ma'am, so I've followed Manny Taubin's career for years. Now that he's a free man, every unattached female in town must be after him. I sure hope he liked me."

"I'm sure he did, Ms. Gaine. Thanks so much for your help."

PART 8

— Chapter 66 —

BACK TO PLAN A, Hallie thought with a sigh. It seemed doubtful that Ms. Gaine had done anything but service Manny and leave. That left the board members, minus Manny and Delsey. The remaining suspects were Melanie Bronstyn, Harvey "Rube" Rubin, Bart Willroch and spouses Efrem Bronstyn and Christina Willroch.

It was safe to eliminate Rube, she decided. Unless he was an amazing actor, his integrity spoke for itself. And Bart was so completely absorbed in himself – and possibly Melanie – he would not be likely to plan and execute a theft.

For the moment, then, she narrowed it down to the two women, Melanie and Christina, since they were the ones Ling would have told about having seen the jewelry box.

Hallie had never met Melanie, but had heard she was an attractive, sophisticated woman with large blue eyes, a slightly long nose, shoulder-length gray-black hair, and exquisite taste. In pictures, she always wore dark colors along with a three-strand pearl necklace. A handsome Michele watch was her only other jewelry.

By contrast, Christina seemed all about glitz, money and labels. Hallie had instantly spotted the Chanel pony hair bag she carried at the gun control dinner. The *New York Times* had featured the purse, priced at $7900 + tax, in an ad. No wonder Bart yelled at her!

Okay, so she loved beautiful accessories and she married a man who didn't like paying for them. She might be able to buy another Chanel purse or two if she could peddle some stolen earrings. But where would she go to sell them?

Chapter 67

A WEEK PASSED, and Hallie was as perplexed as ever. Her brain worked overtime trying to pin the theft on various persons, none of whom turned out to be suspect.

Christina Willroch was always in the back of her mind. If she was guilty, she wouldn't be foolish enough to wear the jewels, but neither had anything turned up in the pawn shops or for sale on the Internet.

A surprise message from Captain Kaiser informed Hallie that Manny Taubin was still paying child support for his 18-year-old son, Deke Taubin Marshall. Under pressure, Manny had agreed to pay his son's college expenses until he graduated or reached 22, whichever came first.

Apparently, Deke Marshall, as he called himself, lived in Portland, Oregon with his mother and stepfather. A recent high school graduate, he would be starting Oregon State University in the fall, working towards a degree in business. He hoped to go on to graduate school if he could save enough money.

An "Independent Advocate" of the Portland Police Department interviewed Deke Marshall, and reported that the young man was not likely to help solve the mystery of Kim Taubin's death.

Should Captain Kaiser so desire, however, the Portland Police would be happy to send her a condensed version of the tape-recorded interview. As soon as Helen received it, she mailed a copy to Hallie.

— Chapter 68 —

CURIOSITY PIQUED, Hallie played the interview that Monday morning as soon as the package arrived. Then she dressed to take Danny to the doctor. The two-year-old had been running a fever since the night before, and his pediatrician agreed to sneak him in between appointments.

By the time the doctor saw him, Danny's temperature had climbed to 103° and she quickly diagnosed a middle ear infection. "It could be serious," she told Hallie. "We mustn't let it spread to the mastoid bone."

Despite Danny's screaming protests, she gave him a shot of antibiotics and sent them home with instructions.

That evening before dinner, Cas held his sleeping son in his arms as Hallie recounted their visit to the doctor. Hearing their voices, Danny stirred and opened his eyes. "Dada?" he said, trying to smile. The medication seemed to be working.

Hallie reached out. "Come to Mommy, darling."

"No!" Danny began to cry. "Dada!" He buried his head in his father's chest. "Bad doctor hurt me. I hate needles!"

Cas patted his head. "It's okay, Danny. It's okay, son. I don't like needles, either." He turned to Hallie. "I'll get Caitlin. She'll calm him down."

Hallie watched helplessly as they left the room. "I love you, Danny," she called. "No one likes —"

She stopped mid-sentence. "Omigod," she said in a whisper. "Danny just solved the jewelry theft!"

Chapter 69

"YOUR SON IS SLURPING ice cream and making a mess in the kitchen. He's quite happy." Cas found Hallie in her office, starting to replay the recorded interview. "May I listen?"

"Have a seat. Here goes..."

A voice boomed into the room:

> "This is four p.m. on Wednesday, May 14, 2014. Robert A. Brady speaking as IA, Independent Advocate for SFPD, case no. 12H-60499876, the unsolved death of Kimberly Wu Taubin on Sunday, March 30th, 2014 at 21 Huntington Court in San Francisco.
>
> Subject of this investigation is victim's 18-year-old stepson Deke Marshall, born Deke Taubin Marshall in San Francisco on 4/12/96.
>
> For this interview, we will refer to the subject as "DM." His mother, Ellie May Marshall Fullerton, has asked to be present.
>
> (Rules, instructions, etc.)
>
> IA: Tell me, Deke, are you here of your own volition?
>
> DM: Hell, no. My mother said I hadda come and tell you what a douche my birth father is.
>
> IA: Do you have a police record?
>
> DM: Hey, man, I read up on you guys. You've already checked me out, Googled me up the yahoo, and know more about me than I do. And you know freakin' well the answer to your question. I had two drug arrests in high school. I've been clean ever since."
>
> IA: Are you angry?

DM: (calmer) Hell, yes. I hadda break a date this afternoon with a hot chick. Pisses me. But I know it's not your fault.

IA: Thanks for understanding. This interview actually saves you from having to fly to Frisco. Tell me, why don't you use your father's famous name?

DM: Are you kidding? He's a dick. My Mom says he used to come visit me when I was little, but now that I've grown up, I've seen him twice. Obviously, he wants nothing to do with me – and vice versa.

IA: What were the occasions when you saw him as an adult?

DM: Both times, I called him to say I was coming to town and could we meet. Both times he took me to dinner at some crummy restaurant where he wouldn't be recognized. And he'd always meet me there. I never went to his house. I never met my stepmother Kim.

IA: Was this before or after your mother sued him for child support?

DM: After. I was 8 years old at the time of the lawsuit, and I hadn't seen Manny since I was a baby. My stepfather had lost his job and my Mom wasn't working. She wanted me to go to a good high school and she wanted Manny to pay for my college. She tried talking to him as a reasonable person but he wouldn't listen. She warned him she'd take him to court. He went ballistic when the story broke in the papers. But that DNA stuff is cool. He couldn't deny paternity.

IA: Did you ever try to contact your stepmother Kim?

DM: What for? She never tried to contact me.

IA: Did you play football in high school?

DM: Yeah, and I made sure no one knew my background. They'd expect a helluva lot more from Deke Taubin than they would from Deke Marshall. Can we go now?

IA: Just two more questions. Now that Manny's lost his wife, will you try to contact him?

DM: Oh, man, no! I told you, he's a dick. For all I know he was glad to get rid of her. Hey, is this an interview or an interrogation?

IA: An interview. How did you first hear of Kim's death?

DM: I read it in the paper. Are we done?

IA: Yes. Thanks for your cooperation and good luck in college."

— Chapter 70 —

SEVERAL SECONDS PASSED. The recording continued:

"This is Robert A. Brady, Independent Advocate. My instant assessment is that Deke Marshall has a great deal of anger and hostility that he tries to hide. He's a nice-looking young man – not as tall as his father – and from the videos I've seen of Manny Taubin, smarter.

In social situations, however, I would guess that he's unsure of himself and uncomfortable. He seems to be afraid that someone might find out his background and be disappointed that he doesn't live up to his father's fame or accomplishments.

His answers appeared to be accurate, yet I felt he was holding back and anxious to get through the interview. There was much he didn't tell us. In general, his nonverbal movements signaled strong discomfort at being questioned.

Signing off at 4:37 p.m."

— Chapter 71 —

"THAT WENT WELL." Cas removed the CD from the computer and set it on his wife's desk. "The kid said nothing, never met the murder victim, has hot pants for some gal – we know where he gets that – and couldn't wait to get the hell out of there."

"It was a bit disappointing." Hallie scratched her ear. "But I agree that Deke was holding back."

Cas nodded. "If we believe this kid, he never met his stepmother, but who knows? And maybe his father really was trying to get rid of her. Or maybe the kid thought his father might pay some attention to him if she were out of the way."

"I'll add Deke to my list of suspects – that is, if Kim was indeed murdered. While we're waiting for the tox screen, I think I'll take Delsey to dinner – alone."

"Alone? You're jealous?"

"When two women want to discuss important matters, they don't want a man around staring at their boobs and having sexual fantasies."

He laughed. "And you never have sexual fantasies about men?"

She pretended to be shocked. "Certainly not! What do you think I am?"

"A liar, darling." He blew a kiss and disappeared.

— Chapter 72 —

"I LOVE GOING to dinner with a female friend," said Delsey de Baubery the next evening. "You can relax and just be yourself. But that's not why we're here, is it. Bring me up to date."

She and Hallie were seated at a small table in the Captain's Galley, a private club overlooking Yacht Harbor and the Golden Gate Bridge. It was shortly before six, and several couples were enjoying the view from the dining room.

"Nothing new about Kim's death," Hallie answered, "but I need to ask you a few questions. If you and Kim were hosting the block party together, and you saw her that morning about 11, and didn't see her again that whole day, weren't you worried? Why didn't you look for her?"

"Are you serious? I looked everywhere! I phoned the house about eight times and got no answer. I rang her bell and no one answered. I called her neighbors who were good friends. I even phoned the guard. Maybe she ran to the store to get something. The guard said he would've seen her if she left, and she hadn't."

"Don't you have a key to her house?"

Delsey wiped a sudden tear. "Of course we have – had – keys to each other's houses. I'll always regret that I didn't

114

go back and use it. You see, Kim was having terrible allergy problems that day. She usually stayed indoors most of February and March, especially mornings when pollens are at their worst. That day she'd been outdoors too long. She was blowing, sneezing, coughing, and her eyes were red. She said she was going home to take double medication and then she'd be back."

"I'm so sorry," said Hallie, gently touching her arm. "I didn't mean to upset you."

"No, no, sweetie, I'm glad you asked. You need all the facts. Poor Kim was miserable. She had a habit of taking off all her clothes and throwing them in the washing machine whenever she'd been outdoors long enough for them to gather pollen. Then she'd take a shower and wash her hair to make sure she wasn't carrying any allergens on her body."

"Do you know if that's what she did that Sunday?"

"I assumed so when she didn't come back. She may have been exhausted – those pills often knocked her out, and she said she was doubling the dose. Or maybe she didn't like the way her hair looked after the shower. I had no way of knowing, and all those neighbors, the caterers, the whole party was my responsibility so I couldn't spend any more time trying to track her down."

"That's most helpful," said Hallie. "We may yet end up with an accidental death."

— Chapter 73 —

THE SERVER INTERRUPTED the intense conversation to set

down two steaming plates. "Enjoy your dinner, ladies."

"Thanks, we will." Delsey brightened. "It would be a huge relief if her death were an accident. We – the neighbors – could stop looking at each other as suspects."

"Given the facts, they're not the only suspects. We recently learned about Manny's son Deke Marshall. Did Kim ever talk about him?"

"You bet." Delsey stopped to sip her wine. "Kim was terribly upset that Manny wouldn't see his son. Manny never forgave Deke's mother for poisoning his reputation, and he transferred a lot of that hostility to Deke. Kim threatened to fly to Oregon and see the poor kid herself, but she never did."

"The Portland police questioned Deke," Hallie said, passing her a written transcript of the interview. "Take a look and tell me what you think."

Delsey read it quickly and handed it back. "Not very productive, I'd say. He sounds mad."

"He is. I know there's something he wouldn't tell us. I'm wondering if he had – maybe some relationship with Manny or Kim that he doesn't want anyone to know about."

"Have you talked to Manny's lawyer, Nate Garchik?"

"About what?"

"Everything. Ask him what Deke is holding back. Also, is Manny leaving Deke any money in his will? When Manny dies, how will he protect his estate against another lawsuit from Deke or his mother?"

"Nate's my lawyer, too. I can't ask him things like that. He'd never breach a client's confidence."

"Nate's a doll, Hallie. He loves women and undoubtedly adores you. Go see him tomorrow and turn on the charm."

116

Hallie laughed. "It wouldn't work. I wouldn't want a lawyer I could charm into telling clients' secrets. But what the heck, maybe it's worth a try."

The women switched subjects over dinner. Delsey admitted her love for Rube but saw no reason to marry again. Hallie updated her on the jewelry theft – except for the final chapter, which was soon to play out.

PART 9

THE NEXT MORNING, Nate Garchik marched through the tall glass doors of Garchik, Dooley & Bechtle LLC and saw a familiar face in the waiting room.

"Well, well. To what do I owe this unexpected delight?"

Hallie jumped up. "No problems, Nate. Nothing's wrong. I know you don't have appointments till 9:00 so I took a chance and came by early. I promise I'll only take five minutes of your time?"

"Is that a question?" He gave her a hug. "Come in, come in, Hallie. Sit down and give me five minutes to get organized. They won't count against your five."

"Thank goodness!"

As she watched him unload his briefcase and start sorting papers, her thoughts raced back to the first time she met Nate Garchik, more than four years ago. She'd had the sad chore of calling on him to report the death of his fiancée. He had never gotten over the loss, and according to mutual friends, worked 12 hours a day and had no desire to get married.

Nor had he changed much; short in stature, deep in voice, expensively dressed, and with the same neat gray moustache and beard. What she remembered most was that first hand shake that conveyed strength and masculinity. Handsome he wasn't, but he didn't need to be. His sex appeal was unmistakable.

Turning his attention to his guest, he settled into a chair. "So, pretty lady, what gives?"

"As you may know, Nate, I'm helping the police solve the death – possibly murder – of Kim Taubin. I understand

119

that her stepson, Deke Marshall, is your client. Without breaking attorney-client privilege, can you tell me anything about him?"

"What makes you think he had anything to do with her death?"

"The Portland police interviewed him for us – for our local police department. He was angry and uncomfortable and seemed to be holding back. I thought maybe you could just tell me if it's worth following that lead?"

The lawyer stroked his beard. "Hallie, my dear, I can't discuss my client. And being the beautiful little snoop I know you to be, you will find out all you can about young Mr. Marshall no matter what I say."

"True. But sometimes I need a push. I'm wondering if I should go to Portland and talk to Deke's friends. Oh, wait! You've given me an idea. Doesn't Kim's sister live in Oregon?"

"I can't answer that."

"Damn you lawyers!" She rose and grinned. "I love you anyway, Nate. Send me a bill for my five minutes."

He pecked her cheek as he opened the door. "On the house, m'love."

— Chapter 75 —

BACK HOME AGAIN, a quick call to Delsey de Baubery confirmed that Kim's sister, Jessica Wu Fong, lived in Salem, Oregon. Hallie found her phone number online, called it and learned it was disconnected with no forwarding number.

Jessica apparently didn't want to be reached, and Hallie

120

decided to respect her wishes. She could always contact Jessica through Manny if necessary.

At the moment, however, she had unfinished business.

After dressing in her favorite Ralph Lauren pantsuit, and adding a handsome emerald brooch Mumsy had given her, Hallie drove downtown. Her shopping list began with six Union Square stores, the best-known and possibly most expensive jewelers in town.

Claiming that she was looking for a pair of diamond and ruby earrings her sister had brought in for repair, she first went into Bulgari, then Cartier, Gump's, Neiman Marcus, Saks and Tiffany.

In all cases, she was asked, "Who made the earrings?" and was politely turned away when she said she didn't know. "We only deal with our own merchandise and our own vendors," was the usual response.

Shreve & Co., however, said they would work on other stores' merchandise, but had no ruby and diamond earrings in their repair department at that moment.

Plan B was to call Helen Kaiser, explain the situation and ask what to do next.

But first, she remembered that her mother patronized a Dutch jeweler named Claude something. He was a favorite of the social set, known to be a brilliant designer as well as being close-mouthed and not likely to discuss his clients or their baubles.

A call to her mother got his full name, Claude van der Meer, a phone number, and his downtown address a block from Union Square. The woman who answered his phone said he was booked solid for the next week, and did she wish to make an appointment for two weeks.

"Couldn't you squeeze me in this afternoon?" she asked. "Please? Mr. van der Meer helps my mother, Edith Marsh. I'll only take a few minutes of his time and it's very important!"

The woman excused herself and came right back. "It's his lunch break but if you can be here in the next half hour, he'll see you. He has a client arriving at one."

"I'll be there in ten minutes," she said.

— Chapter 76 —

NERVOUSLY, Hallie hurried up Stockton to Sutter Street, where Claude had his small boutique. Nestled between a high end baby shop and a designer shoe store, Claude's front door had no sign, no name, no address on it, simply an engraved placard that read, "By appointment only."

Not even a phone number! How exclusive can one get?

He did, however, have a sparkling diamond necklace in his window. Probably cheaper to buy the whole building, she thought.

Two eyes peered through the peephole in the door – then it opened.

"Hello, Ms. Marsh," said a pleasant voice.

A suntanned, white-haired man, probably in his 60's, greeted her with an outstretched hand. "You're just as attractive as your mother says. She's told me much about you. I'm Claude."

"Nice to meet you, I'm Hallie." A quick glance around the shop told her he shared her distaste for clutter. A pair of Mies van der Rohe Barcelona chairs, a Lucite table with a copy of Town & Country, and a glass-topped counter were the main furnishings.

"I hope you're not arresting me," he said, taking her arm and leading her across the room. "Your mother says you like to solve murders."

She smiled, "I do. But I also believe a person's innocent until proven guilty."

He stationed himself behind the glass and set down a black velvet-covered tray. Do you have something for me to look at?"

"No, there's been a robbery. May I talk freely?"

"Would you like to sit down?"

"No, thanks. This won't take long." She described the theft in brief terms, wondering if he happened to receive a pair of ruby earrings to repair or redesign.

"I couldn't possibly answer that question," he said, his warmth suddenly cooling. "Did your mother not tell you I never discuss my clients?"

"Yes, she did. But a crime's been committed. And my question only requires a yes or a no."

"My clients trust me and I honor that trust with my life, Ms. Marsh. I don't mean to be rude, but I've someone coming in ten minutes and I space my appointments so they won't see anyone they know."

She wanted to ask if that was necessary, but realized that some people used him to sell their jewelry, make faux copies of it, or had other matters they wanted kept private.

"I understand, Claude. I appreciate your seeing me."

His charm came back as she headed for the door.

He opened it. "I made that emerald brooch for your mother many years ago. It looks lovely on you."

He closed it before she could thank him.

— Chapter 77 —

BACK IN HER CAR, Hallie drove directly to the police station in the Hall of Justice. With a quick wave to the officers at the front desk, she headed down the hall to Captain Kaiser's office.

The Captain was in a meeting, she learned, but she was welcome to wait.

Forty-five minutes later, Helen materialized.

Hallie rose quickly. "I know, I know, I'm supposed to call first but this can't wait."

She spilled out her story, her visits to the stores, her meeting with Claude. "I'm 99 percent sure who our thief is, and I'm equally sure that Claude has the earrings. I'm just afraid he might feel obliged to warn his client of my visit."

"You think Claude might be a fence?"

"It's worth looking into."

"I'm faxing the theft report to the Property Crimes Division," she said, scribbling a note. "And I'm sending you there to update them. I'll mark it 'Urgent!'"

Chapter 78

SPURRED INTO ACTION by Hallie's visit and Captain Kaiser's request, the Investigations Lieutenant sent two officers to call on Claude van der Meer. The next morning, Helen called Hallie. The police had questioned Claude and released him. At that moment, they were on their way to pick up their suspect.

"How did you know who it was?" asked Helen.

"At first, by process of elimination," Hallie recalled. "Then remember when you sent me to that Gun Control dinner and I saw Christina there?"

"So?"

"We chatted in the ladies' room. When Christina told me she couldn't tolerate needles, I noticed that she didn't have pierced ears. I didn't think much about it till two days ago, when Danny screamed that he hated needles. That started me thinking. If Christina hated needles, and if she had the jewels, and knew better than to try to sell or pawn them, what was left but for her to wear them?"

"Aha!" Helen's eyes lit up. "And if so, she'd not only have to redesign them so they wouldn't be recognized, she'd also have to convert the pierced earrings to clip-ons."

"Precisely. When Manny confirmed that Kim did have pierced ears, I felt I was on the right track. At first I thought Christina might go to Tiffany or Cartier, but when I learned they only repair their own jewelry, I thought of Claude, the darling of the social set. But he's as tight-lipped as the lawyers. How in the world did you get him to talk?"

Helen laughed. "Elementary, my dear Watson. With

some persuasion from my officers, Claude picked out Kim's earrings from pictures of five similar ones, and Manny confirmed by fax that those were indeed the missing pair. We threatened a search warrant for Claude's files, so he was virtually forced to tell us who gave them to him to redesign and repair. Luckily, he hadn't started working on them yet. We had to confiscate them for evidence, but Manny will eventually get them back."

"Whew! Good work!"

The Captain continued, "You'll love this. Christina insists she took the jewels out of loyalty to her 'dear friend' Kim."

"Seriously?"

"She says she took them to keep Manny from giving them to his girlfriends. She aso claimed she was having the earrings repaired so she could donate them to a charity auction. Is that noble or what? Great teamwork, Hallie. Stay in touch."

PART 10

— Chapter 79 —

NATE GARCHIK earned his pay convincing the Judge that his client, Christina Willroch, was full of remorse. It was a first time offense, no one was hurt, Manny would get the earrings back, and all would soon be forgotten.

The Judge agreed that Christina seemed sorry that she was caught, although not repentant about the crime. However, she probably was not a menace to society. So rather than lock her up, he hit her with a $300,000 fine and 450 hours of community service at a homeless center. Volunteering for the Ballet, Opera, Symphony or art museums did not count.

Unable to deny her guilt, Christina pleaded no contest to grand theft larceny. She admitted that Ling, her housekeeper, had indeed peeked inside the jewelry box and related its dazzling contents.

Out of curiosity, and bored by the board meeting, Christina had slipped upstairs to sneak a look at the earrings. What evil force made her impulsively tuck the box in her purse, she'll never know.

Unfortunately for the Willrochs, someone tipped off the *Chronicle* and the story of the theft made the back page. Hallie managed to keep her name out of it, but Bart was horrified, and promptly filed for divorce – which everyone who knew him assumed he'd wanted to do for ages.

Finally he had an excuse to get rid of his most expensive and least profitable asset. If only he'd married with his brain instead of his sex organ. Thank God they had no children!

Chapter 80

THE FOLLOWING MONDAY, while Bart and his lawyer were trying their best to wangle a quickie divorce, Melanie Bronstyn was driving to the flower mart to buy pink hydrangea plants for a client's housewarming. Questions raced through her mind.

Bart Willroch topped the list. Her longtime lover was soon to be a free man, after years of insisting that he wanted to marry her but couldn't afford a divorce. Would his great love suddenly dissolve in his desire to find someone younger, prettier, richer? And if not, why wasn't he answering her emails?

In the unlikely event Bart did ask her to become his wife, did she want to marry him? What about her own marriage?

Most of the time, Efrem reminded her of a big lovable bear. Now that he could no longer perform sexually, he was sublimating his libido in painting and sculpting nude bodies, mostly female. And that was fine with her.

At the same time, he'd been a good husband. To her knowledge, he'd never been unfaithful; rather, he was passionately loyal and hated to see how unhappy Kim made her. Once he'd even called on Kim and tried to talk sense to her about the damn cherry trees. He'd found her stubborn and unpleasant.

A troublesome suspicion haunted Melanie. Knowing how hostile Kim was, could Efrem possibly have played a part in her death? After all, Kim had been a life-size pest to the Bronstyns, and toxic to their marriage. Kim's irritating behavior, in fact, had driven Melanie right into Bart's arms for solace. Or so she liked to rationalize.

At the last board meeting, she remembered, Manny had mentioned some new medication Kim was taking. He was highly optimistic, and said that it might take a few months to work, but then Kim would no longer be allergic to the cherry blossom pollens, and they could all be friends again.

Sure, thought Melanie, and I've been asked to dine at the White House.

— Chapter 81 —

TUESDAY, May 27th, a few days later than expected, was the day Kim's family, friends, and the police had been waiting for. That afternoon, Lenny Brisco called Hallie.

"We got the autopsy report," he announced. "Not much different from what we'd already observed at the scene."

"Tell me!"

"No sign of forced entry, no bruises, no defensive wounds, so if any indications of personal attack had been found, it would have been someone she knew."

"But they weren't found."

"Right. The tox screen showed herbs, vitamins, antihistamines, let's see… 'Cetirizine Hydrochloride, Pseudoephedrine Hydrochloride, more stuff I can't pronounce…'peripheral eosinophilia suggest a hypersensitivity reaction…facial pruritus…' "

"Itching."

"Yeah, apparently she had hives, and itched so bad she scratched her own face…'signs of possible allergic reactions

130

or alteration of immune regulation following candida infection…'"

"Poison?"

"No trace of toxic chemicals."

"Conclusion?"

"Damn it, Hallie, nobody seems to know. It's all doctor talk."

"Read me the ending?"

"Okay, sure. '…myocardial infarction and multiple organ failure, increased microvascular permeability and acute pulmonary edema…' "

"Is there a decision?"

" 'At this time, the Medical Examiner suspects the death to be a suicide due to asphyxia, but a comprehensive investigation must be completed before a final determination is made.…however, no specific macroscopic findings are present at postmortem examination…mode of death is often the result of shock rather than asphyxia. Absence of postmortem findings does not exclude the diagnosis of anaphylaxis…' "

"Anaphylaxis? That's a fatal allergic reaction. Does Dr. Toy think the cherry blossoms killed her?"

Lenny broke into laughter. "Damned if I know."

"What did he write on the death certificate?"

"He had to classify her death as 'Natural, Accident, Homicide, Suicide or Undetermined.' He saw no conclusive signs of homicide or suicide. She didn't die of disease or old age, so it wasn't natural, and it could be accidental, but there were no bruises, no indication of bodily trauma, such as falling down stairs. He had no choice but to classify her death as 'Undetermined.' "

Chapter 82

THE AUTOPSY REPORT did not bode well for the prospect of finding Kim Taubin's killer. By now, Hallie was convinced that the weird circumstances of her death, the number of people with motives, including several neighbors who had strong reasons to want Kim out of their lives, indicated homicide.

Without police support, however, she was at a loss. Captain Kaiser's explanation that they would keep the case open for a while, but would focus their efforts elsewhere, did little to cheer her up.

That evening, after dinner and hugging Danny goodnight, Hallie and Cas settled on the bedroom sofa.

"Maybe you should let this case go, honey," he said, clicking on the television. "If the coroner calls Kim's death undetermined, it means they've covered the bases, and didn't find any indications of foul play."

"I know," she said, "but I can't stop now. There's something out there staring me in the face, I'm sure of it. Say… isn't that the Senator on the screen?"

Cas turned up the sound on the news. A video from the previous evening showed Anna Steinberg speaking at a ceremony honoring Memorial Day, and urging the country to support the veterans of all wars."

"Well said, Senator. We can't do enough for our vets."

Hallie nodded agreement. "She's so attractive and eloquent. Did you ever find out why she sold her house?"

"No." He lowered the sound. "Some man in her press

office told me that was a personal matter, not for publication. I said that was nonsense. She's a public figure and it was well-known that she'd lived in a large house in Huntington Court and recently moved to another large house on the Gold Coast. What do the neighbors say? They must know something."

"I haven't asked anyone."

"Not even Delsey?"

"Ha! I knew you were going there. If you should happen to want to call on Ms. Delsey I'm going with you."

"Darling, how wonderful! You're jealous."

"Let's say I'm practical. I prefer to deal with only one dead body at a time."

PART 11

HALLIE WASN'T really jealous, she thought the next morning as she dressed for the day. She and Cas had a wonderful marriage in so many ways, they both knew they were attractive to others, but neither had felt the need to look elsewhere for sex or solace.

Still…what was that Oscar Wilde quote? "I can resist everything but temptation." So why push it?

The realization that she was uncomfortable having her husband meet with a gorgeous single woman – alone, in her own house – made her feel ashamed and petty. And yet, one can't deny one's feelings.

She reached for the phone.

Delsey answered. "What's up, Hallie? I haven't wanted to bother you, but I'm dying to know what's happening. Any news about Kim?"

"Nothing substantial. I keep getting new suspects."

"Who's on your list so far?"

"Got a minute?"

"I'm all ears."

"I'll try to be brief: There's Dr. Andy Bradstreet, who loved Kim, and said he felt 'stabbed' when she married Manny. It could be one of those, 'If I can't have you, no one will!' situations."

"There's Melanie Bronstyn," Hallie continued. "Apparently she and Kim fought like wildcats over the cherry blossoms. Zelda Rhinehart thought that Kim's book would mention her sons in prison, and I've since assured her it won't. Bart Willroch knows Kim named his architect and it wasn't Willis Polk, which will cost him several million if he decides to sell his house."

"And that's worth killing for?"

"Nothing's worth killing for, Delsey, but you do have weird – unique, anyway – neighbors. What I've gleaned from chatting around is that Efrem Bronstyn knows his wife Melanie's been hooking up with Bart. Efrem blamed Kim for causing his wife so much grief that she flew into Bart's arms, and that affair has – understandably – been toxic to his marriage."

"You have been snooping!"

"You bet. And I assume you and Rube are…"

"Steamier than ever. I'm mad for that man. Is he a suspect, too?"

— Chapter 84 —

"HE COULD BE A SUSPECT," Hallie answered gently. "He feels Kim was responsible for his wife's death, but I don't think he's a murderer."

"Whew! That's a relief. Am I a suspect?"

"You would be if you had a motive." Hallie chuckled. "Somehow I know you'd never risk having to encase that beautiful body in one of those awful orange prison suits."

"Good point! What about Manny?"

"Kim was very much alive that Saturday night when she drove him to the airport and then drove home. The police always suspect the husband first, so they confirmed that Manny was on that particular flight, stayed at the hotel

136

overnight, made a commercial Sunday morning, checked out that afternoon and flew home. To our knowledge, he and Kim had a good marriage. He had no motive."

"Don't you think infidelity's a motive?" asked Delsey. "Maybe he killed Kim to keep her from killing him."

"A lot of husbands screw around when they travel. From what I've seen, the wives often suspect what goes on but close their eyes to it because they want to stay married. I assumed that was Kim."

Delsey sighed. "She knew about it all right. She knew he was a hound dog when she married him. She'd joke about it. He didn't need to kill her. He already had the freedom to indulge his weakness."

"In any case, Manny was out of town and nowhere near Kim when she died or was murdered," Hallie clarified. "I think I told you that Manny has a son, Deke, whom he managed to ignore for 18 years, except for supporting him. Deke hates his Dad with a passion and might have sneaked into his house and poisoned the wrong person – except that the tox screen came back negative for poisons."

"That's quite a list, Hallie. Hard to believe any of those people are capable of murder. Maybe you should start looking for someone outside of Huntington Court."

"That's possible."

"Are you thinking of giving up the investigation and leaving it to the police? I know Cas wants you to."

How did she know that? "Umm – yes, he does want me to forget it, but I've still a lot of snooping to do."

"Then more power to you, Superwoman. Go for it!"

"Thanks, Delsey. Talk to you later."

137

— Chapter 85 —

THE MINUTE she clicked off, Hallie realized she'd forgotten the reason she'd called Delsey – to find out if she knew why Senator Anna Steinberg had moved out of Huntington Court. That way she could tell Cas whatever she learned, and he wouldn't have to contact Delsey at all.

Emotion, however, had taken over and she'd forgotten her quest. And now she had something new to worry about. How could Delsey know Cas had asked her to stop working on the case unless they'd talked recently?

Delsey had said that her relationship with Rube was steaming hot. Was that to throw Hallie off track? What was happening? Was Cas having an affair? Was she – Hallie – being paranoid? Was her imagination going wild?

No, she decided, she wasn't imagining things. True, Cas was trying too hard to make a story out of Anna Steinberg's move. The Senator saw a house she liked better – hardly breaking news. Was it just an excuse for Cas to call Delsey? Nothing seemed to make sense anymore. For a quick second, she felt as if her world were falling apart.

The feeling disappeared almost immediately. Don't be an ass, she scolded herself, stop imagining things. Cas was the sweetest, most thoughtful person she'd ever known. All she had to do was wait till he came home and ask him. Looking her in the eyes, he wouldn't lie to her. Of that she was certain.

But how to approach him? And wasn't she foolish to be wasting so much time worrying about it?

Chapter 86

THE DAY WAS SUNNY, and Mumsy (you didn't dare call her "Grandma" or she'd bite your head off) and Caitlin had taken Danny to the Zoo, leaving her alone in the house. What could she do, she wondered, to stop thinking about Cas?

The answer came with a ring of the phone.

"It's me again," said Delsey, "and for a change I have good news. Kim's book galleys just arrived and they look terrific! You did a fantastic job tying up loose ends. It's a true art book and it started me thinking. Some people love paintings, others prefer sculpture, and so on. But architecture manages to combine all the tangible arts. You can see, feel, touch, embellish…buildings, bridges, towers, houses."

"The difference," she continued, "is that art is for art's sake, whereas architecture is responsible to someone – it has to please someone. And in this case, I think the residents will be thrilled with the book."

"That's great news!" Hallie sprang to life. "May I see the galleys? We're sure to find a typo or two. You're not showing it to anyone else, I hope?"

"I was thinking of having my assistant Francie make a copy of each page and sending it to the homeowner it's about. That way they can proof it and we won't make major boo-boos."

"Don't mean to interfere, but that would be a huge mistake." Hallie spoke fast. "You mentioned wanting to please the residents. When I was in PR, I learned one steadfast rule from the journalists I worked with: You never ever show copy – before it's printed – to the person or persons you're writing about. Sure, they might find a typo or an error or two, but mostly, they'll have you adding facts, changing sentences, deleting stuff, and practically rewriting the whole damn article to make themselves look better."

"Are you sure?"

"In your case, they might even want to change the picture of their house. Of course there are exceptions. Because I was a publicist and not a journalist, I was being paid for writing press releases and I had to please my clients and make any changes they wanted. There were always alterations, some good, some bad. But you don't have to show the book to any of the residents. With a few exceptions, the homes were built years ago and the architects have already pleased the clients who hired them, not to mention the people who bought their houses. Does that make sense?"

"Frankly, not much." Delsey sounded unhappy. "Don't people have the right to see what we're going to publish about them?"

"Hmmm. I don't know the legal answer. I know that if they agree to be interviewed on condition they get to approve the copy before it's printed, we'd have to honor that agreement. To my knowledge, though, Kim never made that agreement with anyone."

"I'd better check with my lawyer, Hallie."

"A brilliant idea. Then you can do as you please."

— Chapter 87 —

SECONDS LATER, Hallie remembered what she'd forgotten to ask. "Before you hang up, Delsey, do you happen to know why Senator Steinberg moved out of Huntington Court?"

"All I heard was that the new house has a much bigger first floor and she does lots of entertaining. Personally, I think she was worried that we were going to turn this into a gated community. As a politician, it wouldn't have helped her image."

Hallie smiled. "That's the whole story?"

"As far as I know. The *New York Times* had a small piece about Congress members' wealth or lack of it. Anna's move was listed with the price she got for selling the house, and what she paid for the new house. I think she sold it for around $10 million and I don't remember anything else."

"That's a good start. We were talking about journalism before, and that reminded me that Cas has a sign on his desk that reads: 'If your mother says she loves you…check it out!'"

"In other words, don't trust anyone, including your own mother? Get the facts yourself?"

"Exactly! Thanks, Delsey, I'll tell Cas it doesn't seem as if there's much of a story there. I'm sure he'll assign a reporter to look into it. He was even going to call you and ask what you knew."

She laughed. "I wouldn't have been much help. Tell him hello for me. Oh, there's the doorbell – must be Rube. We're off to Napa for the day. Oh, wait! Rube said you might want to know that about a week before Kim died, he saw Efrem coming out of her house one Sunday evening around nine. She was very much alive and Rube knew Manny was away. I can't see Kim shtupping Efrem, but what in God's name was he doing there? Darn, there's the doorbell again. Rube's as anxious to get going as I am!"

141

"How wonderful. Have a happy time."

"I'm blissful, Hallie. We're two lovebirds, just like you and Cas. I'll have Francie drop off the galleys. Make any changes or corrections you want, then get it back to me as soon as you can. I'm hoping we'll have the books out before Christmas."

— **Chapter 88** —

To say that Hallie felt ashamed of herself for thinking Cas was misbehaving, would be an understatement. Delsey's comment about Lovebirds touched her, and brought her back to earth with a thump. How could she have questioned such a caring, devoted father and husband as Cas? She would try to be especially loving to him tonight.

And how could she possibly have suspected her good friend Delsey, who was so open and direct about everything? Delsey had even mentioned once, that after having been married to Ashton Crocklebank, she had new appreciation for monogamy, and the value of honest communication between lovers.

Having scolded herself sufficiently, Hallie could get back to the problem that was perplexing her; Kim's death was more of a mystery than ever.

Next on her agenda, she decided, would be a visit to the Bronstyns. Having never met Melanie, she shared Rube's curiosity. What was Efrem doing coming out of Kim's house on a night when Manny was out of town?

But what excuse could she have for calling on them? Ah

– why not the book galleys that just arrived?

— Chapter 89 —

MELANIE BRONSTYN answered her phone that afternoon; she'd be delighted to meet Hallie. In fact, she was home checking a long list of credit card bills and wishing she had an excuse to do something – anything – else.

Dressed to perfection in a navy cashmere turtle-neck over matching slacks, she opened the front door. Hallie recognized her "trademark" three-strand pearls, and in fact, Melanie looked exactly like her pictures – slim, with wide blue eyes, a slightly sharp nose, and gray-black hair superbly coiffed.

"Your home is as elegant as you are," Hallie observed, as they passed the Bronstyns' living room. What a contrast to Christina Willroch's house! Both women collected antiques, but Christina overloaded her rooms with a mixture of fine and not-so-fine pieces. Melanie's furnishings were few and fabulous.

"Appreciate the compliment," said Melanie. "As you may know, decorating's my profession. Let's chat in the library. You say you have the proofs of Kim's book?"

The woman was definitely a pro. No small talk for her. Hallie reached into her tote bag and drew out the galleys.

"Here you are," she said. "I've marked your page – 17."

They sat down beside each other on a black leather couch. To Hallie, the "library," with its pale grasscloth walls, antique hunting etchings and built-in bookshelves, seemed almost too perfect to be warm and cozy.

Above a granite fireplace, a full-length portrait of the hostess dominated the room. The letters "EFR" in the lower right corner left no question as to who painted it.

"Beautiful portrait," said Hallie. "Dare I ask – are those Birkenstocks you're wearing in the picture?"

"How kind of you to notice! My Arizona Slide Sandals have been the rave ever since Celine showed a fur-lined version in his Spring 2013 show. I'm rather fond of that painting," Melanie continued. "Efrem can be quite talented when he sticks to faces."

She slipped on her granny glasses, peered down at the papers in her hand and read aloud:

"The Bronstyns, Melanie and Efrem, are both highly successful in their fields: Melanie, a sophisticated interior designer has won many awards, as has Efrem, a world-acclaimed painter and sculptor. They bought this 1909 Charles Dailey-designed home in 2002. It features a slanted hip roof with projecting eaves…"

The rest of the description she read to herself, then said, "Thank God you didn't mention Efrem's nudes! I've been sick with worry about this book. Efrem's so talented, I hate to have people think he only paints naked ladies."

"You were one of four couples who didn't want to be interviewed," Hallie reminded her. "But we couldn't leave you out, so I'm pleased that you're pleased. Would you have a few more minutes to talk about a less pleasant subject?"

— Chapter 90 —

MELANIE FROWNED. "That would be Kim Taubin, no doubt. I understand you're helping the police find her killer."

"We're not sure she was murdered," said Hallie. "But yes, we're trying to find out why she died."

"I've no doubt that she was murdered. I would've liked to murder her myself at times. I take no pleasure in speaking ill of the dead, but she was the most self-centered, rude, spoiled, selfish woman I've ever known. A disgrace to our gender! I didn't kill her, but it's no loss to humanity. And that Manny person she married is so crude. If that sounds snobby, it is. I don't care how many millions they have, the Taubins did not and do not belong in Huntington Court!"

"What about the good Senator Steinberg? Were you friends? Were you sad to see her leave?"

"We were acquainted. As Ecclesiastes said, 'There's a time for everything.' Anna had always wanted a house with a view. Her generous husband saw a beautiful mansion come on the market, and he bought it for her for her birthday."

"Sight unseen?"

"Unseen by the Senator. When he showed it to her, though, it was love at first sight. Anna had never had time to be involved in the politics of the circle, and she had little emotional attachment to the neighbors. So there were no qualms, no regrets about moving away."

"And you know this because…?"

"I know this, Ms. Marsh, because we share the same hair-stylist, and she gets all the local gossip before it happens." Melanie chuckled as she spoke. "Is there anything else I can

145

help you with today?"

"One last question or two going back to Kim. Were you at the block party the day Kim died?"

"Good Lord, no! We don't go to block parties. And in fact, we were in the Hamptons that week. Forgive me, but I have no desire to mingle with the hoi polloi."

Hallie refrained from asking, "How do you really feel?" Instead, she said, "Does Efrem agree with you?"

"Indeed he does. He hated seeing me so upset about Kim. He even went over to see Kim one evening and tried to talk sense to her. She practically threw him out of the house."

"Would that have been a Sunday evening about nine?"

"I can't remember the day. It was after dinner, yes, about nine." Her eyes widened in surprise. "Don't tell me someone saw him leaving her house and assumed that —?"

Seeing Hallie's discomfort, she burst into laughter. "Forgive me, Ms. Marsh, but my dear husband couldn't have an affair even if he wanted to. And even if he wanted to, I assure you Kim Taubin would not have been on his list!"

— Chapter 91 —

"THAT WAS INFORMATIVE – not," Hallie sighed to herself as she drove home. The realization that Melanie had led the conversation and said little that could help her solve the case, was disappointing. And yet, it was another opinion to tuck away.

Since no one knew why or how Kim died, the fact that

146

the Bronstyns were on the East Coast the day of the block party, proved nothing. Later, however, it might either clear or indict them.

That evening, over their take-out Chinese dinner, Hallie paused to set down her chopsticks. "I talked to Delsey today," she said.

Cas shrugged and poked a bite of pork. "So?"

"She and Rube are going away together for a week."

"So?"

"So she mentioned that you wanted me to quit the case. When did you tell her that?"

He looked up angrily. "You going to start that crap again? I have neither seen nor spoken with Delsey since the last time we saw her together however many weeks ago that was. You must have told her that yourself."

Hallie glanced at him and he stared back. "Okay, sweetheart," she finally said. "I'm sorry. I could easily have said something to her and forgotten. If you didn't have grease all over your mouth I'd kiss you."

"If you loved me, you'd kiss me anyway," he said puckering up.

She laughed, wiped his lips with a paper napkin, then kissed him. "I'm sorry," she repeated. "I also called on Melanie Bronstyn."

"Did you like her?"

"She's a walking ice cube. What does Bart Willroch see in her?"

"Who cares?"

"Not I. I also found out that Anna Steinberg's husband

bought their new house to surprise his wife. Apparently, the Senator always wanted a view. That seems to be the main reason she moved."

"The two-legged ice cube told you that?"

"She did, indeed. She and Anna share a hairdresser."

"What a wonderfully reliable source! Well, so be it. That's actually helpful, and I can tell my reporter to stop trying to dig up something newsworthy there."

"Good," Hallie said, wiping his mouth again. "Pass me the noodles?"

— Chapter 92 —

THE CLOCK said almost nine that evening when the phone rang in Hallie and Cas's bedroom. Cas answered, only to hear a furious voice shout in his ear.

"It's Bart Willroch," he screamed, "and I'm going to sue the ass off that fucking wife of yours!"

Cas smiled sweetly and handed Hallie the phone. "It's for you, darling."

"Hello?" she said.

"Hallie Marsh, this is Bart Willroch. If you publish that goddamn bleeping book Kim wrote, I'm going to sue the pants off you!"

"Please calm down, Mr. Willroch," she said raising her middle finger to Cas. "I'm happy to discuss whatever's making you so unhappy."

"What do you think's making me mad?" he growled. "Willis Polk designed our house, and no one else. I don't know where you got that other jerk's name."

"From court records," she answered. "They don't mention Polk anywhere. James Haeberly designed your house. He was a fairly well-known architect."

"The hell he was! I have signed documents from other architects…"

"Bring them over tomorrow and I'll be happy to look at them," she said. "I assume you spoke with Melanie today."

"She's mad as hell, too."

"She didn't mention anything to me," said Hallie. "This needn't be a problem, Mr. Willroch. Suppose I leave in Mr. Haeberly and just add a line saying that some people attribute the design of your beautiful home to Willis Polk, but that hasn't been authenticated. If you were to try to sell your house as a Willis Polk house, you'd be found out in five minutes and shipped off to jail for fraud."

Long silence on the other end. "Well, why don't you just take me out completely? I don't even want to be in the friggin' book."

"If that's your wish, I can do so. But this is going to be a gorgeous and very popular coffee table book. For you not to be in it will greatly reduce your home's value."

"Shit," he said weakly. "Then leave me in. Now read me the paragraph about us again – what's that sentence you're going to add?"

— Chapter 93 —

HALF AN HOUR LATER, they finally agreed on the addition.

Bart Willroch's reaction made Hallie regret that she'd shown the galleys to Melanie. She must have memorized the paragraph about her lover and phoned him right away.

How stupid Hallie was to ignore her own warning never to show people what you've written about them before it's published! Why hadn't she taken her own advice?

Quickly adding the well-worked-over sentence to the Willroch paragraph, and fearful that Bart or Melanie would call and want to change it again, she wrapped the galleys in a box.

Early the next morning, she mailed them back to the publisher.

Later that day, checking her messages, she found a short text from Captain Kaiser: "Deke Taubin Marshall in town, may call you."

"That's all I need," she murmured. Caitlin had taken Danny to the park, and she lay down for a rare nap. Her eyes had barely closed when the doorbell startled her. Grabbing a robe, she peeked out her upstairs window and saw a red car parked in her driveway. It was new, shiny, and had an Oregon license plate. Who else could the driver be?

— Chapter 94 —

EXCHANGING her robe for a T-shirt and slacks, Hallie ran a quick brush through her hair, applied a dash of lipstick, then headed downstairs to answer the door.

Her visitor was instantly apologetic. "I'm Deke Marshall.

You know, Manny Taubin's bastard son?" the young man said. "I hope you don't mind my bargin' in like this."

"I don't mind at all, Deke." She opened the door and ushered him inside. "I was just going into the kitchen for a pot of tea. It's not too exciting an offer, but would you care to join me?"

"I'd like that!" He beamed eagerly and melted into a smile – his Dad's smile.

"I know you and Manny haven't been close," Hallie said, filling a kettle and pointing her guest to a stool at the counter. He was neatly dressed in a fresh white shirt and khaki slacks, and bore little resemblance to his father.

"You don't look much like him," she continued. "You both have the same dark hair, you're both fairly tall and slim, although you're better-looking. Your face is rounder and friendlier, and your eyes look at a person directly. Best of all, you don't have that awful black beard or all those bulging muscles."

"I sure hope not. I want nothing to do with him. I guess you heard that tape I made. My Mom gave me hell for my language. Sorry if I offended you."

"You did sound rather hostile. You seem like a different person." Hallie handed him a cup of hot water with a teabag on the saucer. "Deke," she said gently. "What brings you here today? Is there some way I can help you?"

"I came to help you, That lady cop, Captain —"

"Kaiser."

"That's the one. She said I should tell you what I told her. She said the police are workin' on the case, but you were like helpin' them and had more time."

"That's true. You never knew Kim?"

"Manny never even invited me to his house. He didn't want me to meet her…afraid we'd be friends and gang up on him or somethin'. He has everyone fooled. They think he's a sports hero, but he doesn't give a blank about anyone but himself. Manny loves Manny."

Hallie's feet began tapping under the counter. "What's your point, Deke?"

"Yeah, sorry, Ms. Marsh. I tend to ramble. Okay, like I told this lady cop, about a week ago I got a letter from a San Francisco lawyer. He said I was named in my stepmother's will on condition that I keep her gift secret and Manny never finds out about it."

"Kim left you some money?"

"Cool, huh, Ms. Marsh? I'm bummed that I can't ever know her or thank her."

"Call me Hallie. Hope you don't mind my asking…was it a large sum?"

— Chapter 95 —

DEKE Marshall squirmed uncomfortably on his stool. "Can I trust you, Hallie?"

She nodded emphatically.

"Fifty big ones! They'll pay for my graduate school. She must've been a saint to put up with Manny. Sure wish I'd known her."

"That's a generous gift."

"My Mom says she felt guilty that Manny wouldn't ever see me. Kim sent me a note with the money saying she hoped I'd make a good life for myself without him. Anyway, I came here for a reason."

"And that is?" Hallie still hoped she might get back to her nap.

"Murder. Kim's note promised she would fly to meet me in Portland so we could get to know each other. She even had plane tickets for when Manny goes to New York in August. Does that sound like a woman who's about to off herself? Manny made her life miserable, but I could tell she was strong – a survivor. The cop lady wants to close the case without finding out what really happened to Kim. Please don't let her!"

"How do you think Kim was killed?"

"Poison. Hadda be. You can find anything online, including stuff that doesn't show up in tox screens. The second and last time I had dinner with Manny he said she was takin' some new medicine for her allergies, and that she was gonna be cured. The cop lady said they'd confiscated all her strange pills and potions – tons of 'em – even the stuff in the fridge – lookin' for poisons. They didn't find any 'cause they weren't lookin' hard enough."

Halie restrained a sigh. "Anything's possible, Deke. I'll be sure to check with the cop lady and make sure they've examined all Kim's herbs and medications."

"Will ya let me know?"

"You bet," she said, relieved that he had finished his tea and was heading for the door. "Nice meeting you, and thanks for stopping by."

Chapter 96

Cas came home that evening, kissed his wife cheerfully, and held up his mobile phone. "Look what I got!" he said. "The police copied my photos and returned my cell."

"Thanks to your old girlfriend, darling," Hallie helped him out of his jacket. "Are we permitted to see the pictures you took at the crime scene?"

"They don't show much, but sure, after dinner. What's thawing?"

"I sent out for Japanese. Delsey and Rube are coming over. He's heard about you and wants to meet you."

Cas's face fell. "I was hoping to get some work done tonight. They won't stay long, will they?"

"You can always excuse yourself. They might be interested to see your pictures, though."

Chopsticks clicked, wine flowed freely, and the tempura was enjoyed by all. Rube and Cas seemed to find endless subjects to discuss, and Cas was no longer in a hurry to get to his work. He transferred the crime scene pictures from his phone to a screen, where they could be enlarged.

Hallie, Delsey and Rube sat on the living room couch as Cas dimmed the lights and picked up a pointer.

"This was my first sight of Kim," he said as a shot of her sandals filled the screen, followed by a view of her lifeless body. The camera moved to the refrigerator, the kitchen stove, then to the cabinets."

"Wait!" said Delsey. "Can you freeze that picture?"

"Sure. I'll even enlarge it."

"Was it taken before the police arrived?"

"Afraid so," said Cas. "I spent about five seconds photographing before I started CPR."

"What caught your eye, Delsey?" asked Hallie.

"The cabinet. If you look closely you can see that the door is not quite closed. In fact, it's open."

"So —?" asked Cas.

"That's the cabinet where Kim kept her EpiPen, the syringe filled with epinephrine," Delsey explained. "A few months ago, she made a special point of showing it to Manny and me, and teaching us how to inject it into her thigh if she ever had a bad allergy attack."

Hallie stared at the screen. "Are you thinking that Kim may have thought she was having an allergy attack?"

"Exactly." Delsey stood and took the pointer from Cas. "As I said, this is where she kept her EpiPen package. If it's still there, that tells us nothing. If it's not there, that suggests that Kim may have opened the cabinet to look for it, and not finding it, collapsed on the floor."

"But who could have taken it besides you and Manny?"

"Anyone, I guess. Perhaps one of the board members. We'd often be in the kitchen searching around for plates or glasses or whatever we needed to prepare a few snacks."

"Would you be able to go to her house and peek into that cabinet?" asked Hallie.

"If Manny's there, we'll stop at 21 Huntington Court on our way home." Delsey signaled a "Let's go," to Rube and blew a kiss to her hosts. "Thanks for a yummy meal!"

— Chapter 97 —

MANNY TAUBIN, congenial as always, was happy to have Delsey and Rube drop by to "take a quick look in your kitchen." He hadn't known that she and the doctor were an item, and seemed pleased with the news.

Aware that anyone, even Manny, could be a suspect, Delsey pretended to open all the drawers and cabinets, stating that she was looking for a silver cup she'd given Kim as a gift. It had sentimental value, she explained, since it was hers as a baby.

A quick glance into the cabinet in question gave her the answer she was seeking. The EpiPen was gone.

Hallie took the news from Delsey as a hopeful sign. Perhaps there was a simple answer to the missing EpiPen. Perhaps there wasn't. Reviewing what she knew, Hallie recalled that Kim had driven Manny to the airport that Saturday evening, March 29th, the day before the block party.

Hallie also remembered that the police had confirmed his stay in Los Angeles, his filming of a commercial Sunday morning, and his late afternoon flight home. As Kim and Delsey had often discussed, he "dated" other women when he traveled, and since Kim wanted to stay married, she ignored his infidelities.

More recently, Deke Marshall's surprise visit had shed new light on himself, his personality, and what he'd been holding back. Almost obsessive about his commitment to keep the news of Kim's bequest from his father, he now had a new cause as well: find Kim's killer.

In person, Hallie realized, Deke was not the angry, hostile teenager in the Portland interview. Wanting to stay out of any discussion that might trigger examining his bank account or involving him with his father in any way, he'd taken pains to sound negative, and to distance himself from his father.

Now, however, he'd had time to think about Kim, and he'd learned to care about her, just as she'd cared about him. His comments on her "strange pills and potions" had not been lost on Hallie.

She knew that Kim had been addicted to her favorite health food store. Delsey clearly recalled hearing about the purple corn chips that would prolong her youthful skin, the cider vinegar that would help regulate her candida issues, the Chinese herbal "cure" for insomnia, even the new medication that was going to end her hay fever forever.

Had the police lab been thorough enough in their investigation of these odd and varied substances?

She would definitely find out.

— Chapter 98 —

THE NEXT DAY, a Friday, Police Captain Helen Kaiser and homicide detective TB were not enthusiastic about Hallie's request for a re-examination of Kim's various herbs and medications.

Under gentle pressure, and because they were friends, Helen finally agreed to review some of the police lab findings.

The lab technicians came back almost immediately, reporting no discrepancies.

Simultaneously, Dr. Toy confirmed that no poisons had been detected in Kim's system or in the contents of her stomach. Hallie specifically asked about the new medication that would "cure" Kim's hay fever. Even though the sublingual drops had been supplied by prescription from a reputable doctor, Hallie begged to take a closer look at the containers.

Reluctantly following his Captain's orders to "humor her," TB called Hallie into his office later that morning and pointed to a series of six small glass bottles on his desk.

"Here's what you asked for, Kim's new medication that we found in her refrigerator," he said brusquely. "Why you're wasting our time with this I'll never know."

Hallie checked a copy of the lab report. "Let's see if I understand how this works: Kim was supposed to start the procedure at least three months in advance of the spring allergy season. She took her first drops on Thursday, March 27th, three days before her death."

"That's right," said TB, as Lenny entered the room and greeted Hallie with a wave. "Each of the six bottles contains samples of the pollens Kim was allergic to. Every morning, for the next two weeks, Kim was supposed to squirt two drops of the weak pollen solution under her tongue. Got it?"

"Yes," said Hallie.

"Okay, pay close attention. Each bottle contained stronger drops than the previous one, and Kim was supposed to take two drops of each strength every day for two weeks. After twelve weeks, her last bottle would supposedly contain enough full-strength solution so she would be fully immune

158

to the pollens. Capeesh?"

"I do." Hallie returned Lenny's wave.

"When you two stop flirting," growled TB, "we'll get back to business. I'm thinking that someone could have switched the labels on these bottles so that instead of taking the weakest solution, Kim took the strongest one."

"Brilliant, TB!" said Hallie who was thinking the exact same thing. "I'd never have thought of that. Could we ask the lab technician to steam off two labels – one on the bottle with the weakest solution and one on the bottle with the strongest – and check for prints underneath the labels?"

Flattered that she liked his idea, TB picked out the first and last bottles and had Lenny rush them to the lab with instructions. Hallie was to come back in an hour.

— Chapter 99 —

TIME DRAGGED as Hallie sat in a waiting area at the police station, making phone calls and scanning outdated magazines. An hour and a half later, Lenny Brisco appeared.

"'Fraid I have bad news," he said. "The only prints under the labels were those of the pharmacist who made the solutions. It was a great idea, but I guess that's that."

"No way, Josè. Not just yet." Hallie paused to choose her words. "Look, Lenny, while I was sitting here, a light went off in my head. What if – instead of changing labels, the perp simply switched the contents? That way, the bottle with the weak drops now had the strong drops."

159

"I get it," said Lenny. "The weak dose she was supposed to take became the strongest dose that she wasn't supposed to take for three months. At that time, her immune system would be built up enough to handle it."

"Bingo! If Kim took the concentrated drops before she was primed for them, she'd have a major allergy attack. And it looks like she did. Worse yet, she told Delsey her symptoms were so bad that morning that she was going to double her medication."

"Oh, no!"

"Lenny, we have to send those two bottles right back to the lab. If they find that the contents have been exchanged... we'll have our murder weapon!"

— Chapter 100 —

THE LAB REPORT came back swiftly. Results were positive. Someone had indeed switched the doses. Back in TB's office, Hallie suggested that the detective call Dr. Toy.

Amazed that such an obvious possibility had been overlooked, the coroner had no trouble confirming that Kim's death could very likely have been due to anaphylactic shock.

"What the hell is that, anyway?" TB asked Hallie.

"It's a sudden, severe reaction of the immune system to an allergen – something like peanuts or pollens that the person's allergic to. If there's no epinephrine or EpiPen available, the person lasts a short time, then goes into a coma and dies."

"In that case," said TB, "I'm calling Toy right back."

Their conversation was brief; TB hung up with a sigh. "Toy says yes, we now have the possible and probable cause of Kim Taubin's death. He's willing to change the death certificate to rule the death a homicide. First, however, he needs a who, a how, and conclusive evidence."

"With your and Lenny's help," said Hallie, "I'm going to try to get it."

— Chapter 101 —

FIRST on Hallie's agenda was to check the footprints in the crime scene kitchen. Cas's five seconds of pictures included one of the body and the surrounding floor. An email to TB confirmed that there were three sets of footprints: Kim's, Manny's, and a third set they hadn't identified. They were small and feminine, and Hallie guessed – correctly, they later found out – that they were Ling's.

Putting footprints aside for the moment, Hallie focused on the EpiPen. If Cas hadn't taken pictures right away, the ambulance drivers dashing through the kitchen would certainly have slammed the cabinet door shut as they rushed by. It was closed in all the later pictures.

Nevertheless, the fact that it was open at the time of Kim's death told Hallie that Kim had undoubtedly been searching for the EpiPen. Had she found it, she'd be alive today.

TB conjectured that she may have forgotten that she moved the EpiPen to a more accessible place. That being a possibility, he would try to get a search warrant for the house.

Chapter 102

ON MONDAY June 2nd, 2014, Manny Taubin reluctantly agreed to let the police comb through his house – not that he had a choice. He had no idea what they were looking for, but felt certain they would find no clues to his wife's death.

They did, however, find a container of oxycodone hidden in a box of toothbrushes in the bathroom. Its significance was uncertain. The second discovery, in Kim's medicine cabinet, hit the jackpot. The top shelf held the EpiPen package which hadn't been there before. Fingerprints on the box belonged to Kim, Manny, and Delsey.

"Unfortunately, that doesn't prove anything," Hallie told Cas that evening. "It's logical that Manny and Delsey might have handled the package when Kim showed them where it was."

"How tall was Kim?" asked Cas.

"About five foot two."

"How high was the shelf where they found it?"

"TB said it was the top shelf. He said they wondered why a short woman would keep emergency medication so high that she'd need a stool to reach it."

"That's your answer, sweetheart. Isn't it obvious that Kim wouldn't have put it there herself? Whoever did put it there didn't want her to be able to reach it."

"What are you saying?"

"What I'm saying is an old journalistic truism: 'Never ignore the obvious.' "

Hallie shook her head. "But the obvious would be Delsey or Manny."

"Exactly," he said. "Take it from there."

— Chapter 103 —

HALLIE WAS QUICK to exclude Delsey as a subject. She had no possible motive for wanting her best friend dead. Captain Kaiser agreed that it might make sense to bring Manny in for questioning. Now that they knew the "how" of Kim's death, they also knew that being out of town proved nothing, and his alibi had little relevance.

After a short chat with Delsey, Hallie drove to the police station where the interrogation already was under way. She stood with Helen outside the room's window, watching and listening.

TB had just finished entering time, date, and other data into the record. Then he let Lenny begin. Their good cop (TB) and bad cop (Lenny) routine was already in place. Manny sat stone-faced, accompanied by Egan Sullivan, the city's best-known criminal defense lawyer.

"We've got you cold, Manny," announced Lenny, pacing the floor with his hands behind his back. "On the evening of Saturday, March 29th of this year, your wife went to see her friend Delsey de Baubery to finalize plans for the next day's block party."

"Alone in the house," he continued, "you entered the kitchen and took two bottles of your wife's allergy medication out of the refrigerator. You poured the contents of the weak solution into a third receptacle, then refilled the weak bottle with the stronger solution. You then poured the weaker

163

solution into the bottle that previously contained the strong solution."

"You guys are crazy," said Manny. "First you wreck my house this morning looking for evidence you didn't find, and now you're makin' up fairy tales. I don't know what the hell you're talking about."

"Be quiet," Sullivan snapped. "I'll do the talking."

Lenny picked up where he'd left off. "Later, that same Saturday night, you let your wife drive you to the airport. You had seen her take her allergy drops that morning and knew she would take them again the next morning while you were in Los Angeles."

"What kind of bullshit is this?" Manny demanded.

Sullivan glowered at him, then told Lenny to continue.

"Okay, fast forward to Sunday. Kim gets up early, she and Delsey plan the day's block party. Kim goes home to take her drops and possibly change her clothes. Amost as soon as Kim takes the drops under her tongue, having doubled the dosage, itchy hives break out on her face. She claws at them, starts to choke, loses her breath, and realizes she's in anaphylactic shock."

Lenny continued, "Panicked, Kim gropes in the cabinet for the EpiPen, and not finding it, collapses and falls to the floor. With no one to help her, she goes into a coma and eventually dies. Pretty smooth plan, Taubin. Did you think you were committing the perfect crime?"

"You don't have to answer that," said Sullivan.

"He's full of shit," said Manny, rising. "I don't have to listen to this."

"I'm afraid you do, Mr. Taubin." TB was right there to

164

take his turn as the good cop, and help the suspect back to his seat.

"My partner, Lenny, majored in acting when he was young," TB explained. "He tends to be over-dramatic. I do apologize if he was offensive. Let's try to go slowly, Mr. Taubin. Are you denying that you switched the contents of the serum bottles?"

"You have no evidence of that," said Sullivan.

"You've seen our evidence," said TB. "You know we have it."

"You have nothing, officer. Zero. Zilch, nothing. Circumstantial at best. Remind me again – what was my client's supposed motive?"

Lenny chimed in: "Any number of witnesses will testify that the famous Manny Taubin is a serial adulterer who badly wants his freedom. We have conclusive evidence that he consulted a top divorce lawyer while in Los Angeles, and learned the exorbitant costs that a divorce would entail. There's no better evidence. If I were a lawyer, I'd tell the suspect he'd do well to confess."

Sullivan whispered in his client's ear. Manny shook his head in an adamant "No!"

"Suppose – just suppose," the lawyer continued, "that my client did change the solutions hoping to scare his wife into thinking her health problems were more serious than they are. He never intended to kill her. Suppose he just wanted to convince her that she shouldn't live in Huntington Court with all the cherry blossoms, and that maybe they needed separate homes. After all, and again, this is pure hypothesis – Kim was the one who doubled the dosage."

165

"What are you blabbing about, Sullivan?" Manny stood up again and TB carefully sat him down. "That's pure bullshit and you know it!"

"Not quite," said Lenny. "Kim's doctor confirmed that in Kim's highly sensitized condition, a single dose of the strong solution would also have sent her into anaphylactic shock. Clearly, fingerprints show that your client moved the epinephrine to a place where Kim couldn't find it and couldn't reach it in time if she did."

"May I have five minutes with my client?"

"Of course you can, Mr. Sullivan," said TB kindly. "Just press this buzzer when you're ready."

— Chapter 104 —

FIFTEEN MINUTES passed before the buzzer sounded. TB and Lenny returned to the interrogation room. Hallie and Captain Kaiser continued to listen and watch. Manny's face was set in a frown.

TB began again. "We heard that Dr. Toy asked you about Kim's allergies and you told him that she was taking shots and getting better. Is that true?"

"Hell, I said they were shots because nobody understands about the drops," said Manny, relaxing his grim expression. "They're too new here, even though they're all over Europe. The drops haven't been FDA approved for curin' allergies in the U.S., medical insurance won't pay for it, and I didn't want to get Kim's doctor in trouble."

"You didn't have to lie, Manny," said Lenny. "The drops

are perfectly legal in the U.S. if they're dispensed by an ENT – an ear, nose, and throat specialist. And Kim's were. We've got you by the short ones, Manny, and you know it. Might as well start telling the truth."

"Okay, the truth is that I did switch the serums," Manny blurted, "but it was only a joke. I meant no harm."

Sullivan looked to his client who shook his head "No" again. Then the lawyer asked Lenny, "What are you offering?"

"Hold it!" said Manny, "You're fired, Sullivan! I want a new lawyer."

TB sighed loudly and waved to the guard. "Get him out of here and take Sullivan with you. Put them in the other interrogation room to cool off, then read Taubin his rights. And Lenny, call the coroner PDQ. Tell him we finally have enough evidence to rule Kim Taubin's death a homicide. I do believe we can close this case."

— Chapter 105 —

CAS CAME HOME early that evening. "We just put the paper to bed," he told Hallie, who was busy mixing a Caesar salad. "Shall we go out to dinner and celebrate?"

"You got my message about the case?" she asked, kissing his cheek.

"I did – and congratulations! I checked with Captain Helen and got the whole scoop for the new issue. We put an old football picture of Manny on the cover. Now that he's admitted he changed the dosage of Kim's drops, his trial's going to be a circus. All his fans as well as several hundred husbands he cuckolded will be there to praise or blast him. I hope you won't have to testify."

"Nope, Delsey's already talked to the prosecutor and she's willing to tell all. Her tales of Manny's escapades, his lies and his selfishness should resonate with the jurors – the female ones, at least."

"Thank the Lord! Now can we please get back to our normal lives again?"

He walked to the counter where she was standing and kissed the side of her neck. "By the way," he whispered, "Danny saw some pictures of Disneyland and he's dying to have us take him there. Would that be spoiling him?"

"I think it's a great idea, darling. We'll take Caitlin along so you and I can have some time to ourselves. You did say you hoped Danny wouldn't be an only child, didn't you?"

"I most certainly did. Not having any siblings would be cruel and unusual punishment." He took the spoon out of her hand and drew her gently to him. "Now – how do we call that travel agent?"

— Epilogue —

AFTER A LONG, drawn-out trial, Manny and his smooth-talking lawyer convinced the jury that Manny had had no intention of killing his wife. He claimed he was convinced that the sublingual drops were mostly apple juice, and he wanted to prove to Kim that the set-up was a scam.

But it wasn't; the pollens were real. If Kim hadn't doubled the dosage, and if she hadn't brought the EpiPen upstairs where Manny moved it to a higher shelf, the disastrous result would never have happened.

Nevertheless, Manny was convicted of "involuntary manslaughter" without "malice aforethought." His five year sentence, according to his lawyer, meant that he'd be out in one. His son, Deke Marshall, graduated from engineering school "with distinction" and became successful in his field. He never saw his father again.

Manny Taubin sold his house to a young Silicon Valley billionaire, and moved to L.A. From then on, the killer's name would rarely be mentioned.

The Willrochs divorced and Bart promptly dropped Melanie for a rich widow. Delsey and Rube had a "commitment" ceremony, but stayed in their own houses.

And Huntington Court? To the residents' delight and surprise, "The Historic Houses of Huntington Court" sold well, thanks, in part, to a series of book parties hosted by the neighbors. With Kim gone, there was no further talk of uprooting the cherry blossom trees.

Little else changed in the privileged enclave. For its residents, Huntington Court would always be the most beautiful living area in the city. For tourists it was a sight not to be missed.

As Melanie Bronstyn once said, "When I wake up in the morning, and look out my window at the sun beaming down on the handsome mansions and spectacular cherry blossom trees…I know I'm the most fortunate person in the world!"

Made in the USA
Las Vegas, NV
30 June 2021